Acclaim for Salar Abdoh and *The Poet Game*

"The novel races through a series of atmospheric settings.... An entertaining and heart-quickening debut."

—*Publishers Weekly*

"Critics pronounced the spy novel dead after the fall of the Berlin Wall: *The Poet Game* shows that it is alive, well, and living in Manhattan. The voice is spare, clean, and insightful. I was reminded of classic noir...and Salar Abdoh captures it brilliantly."

—Eoin McNamee, author of *Resurrection Man*

"Abdoh has obviously done his homework. His precision depicting New York City streets is almost spooky."

—Fox News Online

"[An] ambitious thriller...a gifted young writer...Abdoh has important things to say about the threat of Islamic fundamentalist terrorism."

—*Ft. Lauderdale Sun-Sentinel*

THE POET GAME

Salar Abdoh

Picador USA ▪ New York

 For information, address Picador USA, 175 Fifth Avenue, New York, N.Y. 10010.

Picador® is a U.S. registered trademark and is used by St. Martin's Press under license from Pan Books Limited.

For information on Picador USA Reading Group Guides, as well as ordering, please contact the Trade Marketing department at St. Martin's Press.
Phone: 1-800-221-7945 extension 763
Fax: 212-677-7456
E-mail: trademarketing@stmartins.com

Design by Michelle McMillian

Library of Congress Cataloging-in-Publication Data

Abdoh, Salar.
The poet game : a novel / Salar Abdoh.
p. cm.
ISBN 0-312-20954-1(hc)
ISBN 0-312-20968-1(pbk)
1. Terrorism—New York (State)—New York—Prevention—Fiction.
2. Iranians—New York (State)—New York—Fiction. 3. New York (N.Y.)—Fiction. I. Title.
PS3551.B2687 P64 2000
813'.54—dc21

99-055845

10 9 8 7 6 5 4 3 2

To my friend and mentor,
Frederic Tuten

The world of espionage was a region of the mad, in which men who could not write or paint or sculpt created distorted works out of the flesh of living persons and said—*believed*—that the result was art.

—Charles McCarry,
The Last Supper

THE POET GAME

1

THE LIBYANS WHO surrounded him were humorless fellows. It was nothing to get restless about, Libyans were notorious for this. In early 1992, when the Office had penetrated the inappropriately named "Lightning Battalion" in a northern Tehran suburb, he'd come in contact with a lot of these so-called Exchange Students from various Arab countries. The Lebanese were hotheads, the Syrians were cautious, old-hand PLO guys were capable of degenerating in a flash, the Egyptians could be serious and smart, yet also egotistical and clownish. But the Lemons, as the Libyans were called, were a breed apart. No talk, little action. And definitely not the kind of *freedom fighter* you'd want to cover your back in times of trouble.

One of the Libyans said something in Arabic and nodded in the direction of the cemetery they were passing. Sami had seen it from high up when the plane had been circling over Kennedy Airport. From this vantage point the sprawling graveyard had a certain authority to it, but from the plane it had appeared as something indecent and incomplete. He thought, How is one supposed to explain this idea to a Libyan brother? Then he wondered if he shouldn't say something for the sake of politeness. Neither of the men in the back responded, however, to his comment about being hungry. Finally the one in the passenger seat, a fleshy character who seemed to be the boss, turned to face Sami.

"It's Ramadan. You don't eat."

The finality of the statement should have piqued him, but he didn't feel up to it. You usually had two sorts of Arab operatives to deal with: one set acted as if having an agent from Iran was like having the Prophet's own right-hand man at the helm, while the other lot were pugnacious and sneering, treating the Persians as if the ancient battle of Qadissiyah between the two races had never ended.

For the time being Sami was content to exert little effort. A more energetic emissary might already have been collecting brownie points trying to please these boys. He tapped the fat Arab who had addressed him.

"What?"

"You speak my language?"

"What, Persian? That's not funny."

"Then I'll say it in English: fuck you; I'm going to eat anyway."

The fat man gave a shrug and the ones in the back shifted uncomfortably. The car sped along a wide street. Sami read "Jamaica Avenue" on a street sign. For no reason that he could think of, seeing this sign made him think of Winston Churchill. There had been a street in Tehran called Churchill, the name of which they'd changed after the revolution. He wondered why somebody would want to call a street in Brooklyn, Jamaica. He could ask the stone-faced Lemons—*Limu* in Persian—but he doubted if it would initiate conversation. He settled back into the seat, wondering if somebody was going to offer him a cigarette so he could refuse—but no, it was Ramadan, month of fasting, and they probably expected him to pray alongside them. This wasn't a comforting thought.

They passed a traffic light as a Hasidic man was getting into his car. This caused stirrings of tension in the car, like the push of a wrong button. The driver, a dark-skinned young fellow with Berber features, muttered something under his breath.

"I always knew I should have learned Arabic when I had the chance," Sami said.

Without turning around, the fat fellow up front repeated the tail end of Sami's sentence, "When you had the chance."

"Yeah, in Lebanon. 'Ninety to '92. I've paid my dues, helped the brothers."

There was more silence while they turned into a side street. Then the big fellow started to ask him about dues. "What is 'dues'? You speak well English? How come?" But he didn't stop for an answer. The four of them slid out of the car at the same time. Sami followed.

It was a three-story redbrick building with a black iron gate that opened to the side of the first floor. The street was nicely tree-lined, and brown-skinned kids played in it. For a second he was scandalized at the apparent amateurism of these people; was this an Arab neighborhood? But then he heard the staccato exchange of Spanish. And soon he was even more relieved as a Chinese woman went pushing a stroller on the other side of the street. This made him recall how little he really knew. Until last week he'd been back to working on one of the Colonel's pet projects in Tehran, mostly translating reveal-all memoirs by former agents of this and that Western intelligence service. For internal consumption of the Office, of course. As if any agency worth a dime would let its real secrets be given away that easily. Nevertheless, it was a job and it beat chasing Interior Ministry guys all over the city.

A big-breasted, light-skinned man with a goatee and a Bokhara cap opened the door, looking rather too self-consciously pious. An American, Sami guessed, searching for Islam's regimented enlightenment.

He found himself in a small room with a barred window boarded up from the outside. A floor mat and an old yellow blanket had been thrown in a corner for him to sleep on. A Koran lay atop a short stool. A closet with no door stood empty save for a few plastic clothes hangers bunched to the side. This was evidently intermission time. How long it lasted was up to the Libyans. He was a houseguest without a key, being welcomed to Brooklyn, New York.

He'd been incarcerated before, but only during routine Office exercises. What was not so easy to figure was whether this, too, was an exercise or not. So on the second day, out of sheer boredom, he began to delve into the Koran they'd provided him with, readying himself for the long haul. They probably had him under some sort of observation, though he couldn't tell how. He gave a name to the man who had received him inside the house—Hazrat, or Prophet—just to fix his face in his own mind. Hazrat set out a food tray for him without saying a word—at an hour which Sami guessed to be dusk—

two days in a row. On the third day Sami tried to break the ice.

"Your hospitality is beginning to weigh on me, brother," he whispered in a sarcastic voice.

The hesitation took the form of Hazrat's setting the tray by the door, and then arranging and rearranging its position as if it were less food than an offering. Sami reached for a piece of sweet date—they were splurging.

"Are you scandalized at me, brother?" he asked as the other was leaving the room.

They didn't give him much of a chance after that. When the door burst open it dawned on him that old Hazrat had forgotten to lock it. Not that he would have tried to get out. Stretching over on the mat, he said in Persian, "Fellows, if you treat your friends like this, I'd hate to visit you at home in Tripoli."

A runt of a Libyan with bushy eyebrows began to yell in Arabic and frisk through his clothes. Two other men stood around, pretending to debate something among themselves. This was the shake-up that Sami had been expecting for some time. He let himself be manhandled until a carefully shaven man wearing a pale blue suit appeared outside of the door.

"Tell the fuck to either shoot me or give me a cigarette," Sami said, again in Persian.

The man in the doorway stepped closer and answered, also in Persian, "But, Mr. Amir, you don't smoke cigarettes."

Sami muttered something to the effect that now they were getting somewhere. The runt shook him again and the man who had answered him in Persian said, "He says you've come here to spy."

"Well, we all have to get to America somehow."

"Just live through it. These Libyans don't trust their own mothers, you know."

The interrogation lasted an hour, during which time the other Iranian supplied Sami Amir with cigarettes which he lit up but didn't smoke. The fat Libyan who had sat in the front seat of the car came in shortly and put the questions to him in English. A second Libyan made as if he was taking notes.

"Your rank?"

"None. Sami Amir, Section Nineteen of Intelligence and Security. Travel orders, none. By the way, I'm hungry." Here was one instance of a cigarette offer. Why was it smokers always assumed anyone could smoke his way out of hunger? "Our aim is zero besides financial backing for fellow Moslem brothers here in the United States. You can ask and I'll communicate it with Tehran. When and if the time comes for anything, Section Nineteen wishes to remain ignorant of the specifics."

"How did you come into the system?"

Sami looked across at the Iranian, who was watching him closely.

"It's all right," the fat man said, looking past Sami at the boarded window. "Colleagues should trust each other at times like these."

"That's a negative. My window, so to speak, at Nineteen remains anonymous. If you're not already aware of that, then you are either terribly naïve or you're a fraud. Either way means I'm done on American soil."

The fat man laughed. "What are these heavy words, Mr. Amir: 'terribly naïve'—you speak English like a Yankee. And you look like one. How come?"

This was a signal that they were now into the "serious"

phase of their vetting and Sami had to give them the rundown of what they already had on him and keep to himself what they didn't. "First off, gentlemen, my mother was an American, although I never met her." Sensing no blatant aversion to this, Sami continued. A few times the fat man stopped to ask questions about things they had already gone over, especially about where he'd picked up his English. So Sami told him about the small Christian missionary–run boarding school in northern Tehran that the father he hardly ever knew had paid for over the years. He leaned into this part of his story, knowing the Arab penchant for collecting heartbreak. He talked of how after the annual stipend at the missionary school had stopped coming, the blind Irish Father O'Malley had decided to keep him on anyway, because . . . well, there was no because; sometimes people just did good deeds because they felt it was the right thing to do.

"Why did you mention Lebanon in the car? You were never in Lebanon from '90 to '92."

"I was testing the extent of your knowledge." Sami paused. He didn't want it to come out as a small victory on his part, but he said it anyway: "And you can't say I haven't succeeded." He offered an inappropriate smile.

The fat man pressed for the sake of argument, "Is it necessary for you to test anything?"

"You're damn right it is." He had meant to work himself into some sort of righteous anger, but now he felt it rising up for real. "Section Nineteen sent me here, not my grandmother. Things are hard enough, and I had to get here on a bona fide visa. My own picture, my own name, passport, the whole works. They said I'd get my instructions across the water. So far all I've got is a slap in the face, hunger, and a gang of suspicious Libyans who seem to prefer to see me vanish. You tell me why?"

The quick outburst made them retreat from his room with a little more grace than they had entered with. The door stayed unlocked. After an hour's worth of soul searching he finally decided to venture out of his hole. The fat man and the Persian weren't there. But three other Libyans were busy practicing karate in the middle of the carpeted living room floor. One by one they stopped what they were doing to stare at Sami. The barrier of language divided these men of apparent common cause, Sami on one side and the Libyans on the other. He noticed the light-skinned Hazrat sitting cross-legged in the corner of the room, reading the Koran loudly to himself with exaggerated intonations. He read too flawlessly to be an American. Maybe he was a Syrian after all, maybe neither.

Sami called out to no one in particular, "I'm going out for a walk; if I don't come back, it's not your fault," imitating the last words of a high-ranking KGB defector to the Americans before the man had redefected to his own people. Sami had had to translate the public version of that story for the Office so the brass could read about it and gloat over hard-to-comprehend CIA bungling. Yet he doubted whether any of the men in this room could quite appreciate the joke even if their English was up to par. So he headed outside and was relieved to find that the night sky here looked no different than it did in most other places he'd visited before.

Hardly a block down the street he came upon a Chinese fast-food joint that cooked *halal* meat. This provoked a double take—a Chinese restaurant that served kosher food for Moslems! Less than a second later a Caribbean whore said something to him in Spanish. He didn't know what she said and couldn't even be certain if she was a whore. Ambiguity everywhere. How did those Libyans handle such everyday encounters in America?

He ended up eating at an Oriental joint down the street. He ordered a dish called "Hot Tofu Over Rice." He left the tofu but ate the rice, though reluctantly. It wasn't very good rice. Not by a long shot.

2

DAMADI'S PLACE was a miniature version of one of those government-owned handicrafts stores you could find all over Tehran. There wasn't just one "exportable" brass kettle but four of them spread over the open counter in the kitchen. At least a half dozen kilims lay on top of one another in a corner of the living room. The silverware was cheap but plentiful—silver tea cups, silver sugar cube containers, and pitchers stacked about like little trophies. The window looked over a tree-lined block of 31st Street on the east side of Manhattan. It was an idyllic, calm winter day outside, sunny and not too cold. Obviously Damadi wasn't pleased about having Sami here and he was doing a bad job of preserving the cool liaison persona he'd put on at the Libyans' house in Brooklyn. He'd traded his blue suit for a cashmere cardigan and looked like a man who was fighting hard not to appear artificial.

"You don't just get up and come to my place," he said, as if reaffirming something that had been going through his mind for some time. "How did you find it?"

"I had an address."

"A note?" Damadi asked, faking too much alarm.

"Hacked into the recesses of my brain," Sami responded. "No one said anything about getting grilled when I got here."

This wasn't a complaint, though he expected Damadi to get defensive about it anyway. As he stood there looking into the other man's face, Sami had a notion that neither of them knew how to be at ease in a professional sense. They were out of their depths around here but had to play along because it beat pushing paper in some dreary office building back in Tehran. Yet secrecy bore heavily on them. Sami could not see spilling his guts to this fellow under any circumstances, but he could see them having a stock chat about the value of the soaring dollar on a rainy day back home—the kind of man you automatically avoid on your next chance meeting by crossing the street.

"His name is Nur," Damadi said. "He's a Pakistani. Another whiz from over there. They say if it had been his job the WTC building would have come undone in half a minute."

Sami sat down. "I have no idea what you're talking about."

Damadi walked over to the cabinet and took out something that Sami would not have expected to see in the man's house: a bottle of J&B whisky. Without making an offer to Sami, he poured for himself in a drawn-out and deliberate manner that was an outright challenge, as if to say: "So what if I work for the security apparatus of the Islamic Republic of Iran; this is *my* place and this happens to be New York City."

He'd seen this attitude in other men of official capacity.

They were borderline bad-boy cases who weren't sure how far they could push with the small perks before someone higher in the hierarchy wised up to them and started to apply pressure.

Damadi looked Sami over. "If you're trying to tell me you were sent here as a blank slate, I will not buy."

"My travel orders were so general I thought I was going on a holiday. If Section Nineteen has you here, then what is the purpose of my holding the purse? And what purse! They tell me to make contact with headquarters and things will be arranged. No wonder those Libyans are suspicious. And now you're mentioning this Pakistani—what was his name again?"

"Nur."

"This so-called whiz boy who needs cash for his gadgets. If a phone call is all it takes to make the Arabs happy, then I'm sure you can punch numbers as well as I can. Right?"

Damadi was smiling. "That's the part that baffled me, too, at first. Forgive me, but it was my idea to hold you for observation for three days. I myself couldn't figure it out either. But you know how they are back in Tehran. They have a weakness for secrets. Now they say you are to provide general whatever."

"That's real helpful information, general whatever."

"I mean do the leg work, shop around, make contacts, promise them money. Besides, you have fair skin, light hair, and your English is like a native. That helps, too. So it's your game with the Libyans. Now I need to know if you were followed."

"It makes no difference. But I was. I thought . . ."

"You thought this is a joint thing, planned through the ranks. But you forget we're in America now. It's better to let things happen a little haphazardly here instead of leaving a trail that's too clean."

Distorted logic, Sami thought. And it smelled bad, too. But he decided not to push it for the time being.

The two men didn't bother with the niceties of a good-bye. Back out on the street Sami began to think. Every time he got sent to a new city he sensed he could get lost forever—which was not necessarily a good thing. Paris and London were the extent of his foreign watch, a few weeks of having to examine the backsides of some parasites from the Oil Ministry in the former city, and two much longer stints in London, where he'd been instructed vaguely to keep an eye on teams of State Security thugs. As if he could have popped up to say, "Stop!" in case those guys ever took it to their heads to do away with an exiled dissident here and there. Fortunately for him, both those terms had been pretty eventless. The Office (being his real employer) wasn't in the business of events anyway. So-called *events* were the specialty of people like those holier-than-thou hoodlums at Section Nineteen. Which was why the Colonel had decided to have Nineteen penetrated in the first place by sending Sami here to pose as one of theirs.

At this point, however, both the Colonel and the Office were too many miles away and Sami didn't feel a bit comfortable being here. Europe might be small, but one at least always had the feeling that help was not too far. Europe was manageable turf, whereas the States were truly foreign country. Plus, this Manhattan grid daunted him. Having done translations of Western intelligence literature in abundance for the Office, Sami was aware that no service worth its salt would send a man away without thorough preparation. Not even those geniuses at State Security did this. But the Office—or

Daftar, as it was called in Persian—being a shadow organization, quite justly claimed lack of manpower. They were the sort of self-proclaimed counter counterintelligence clique with which the State Security people in Iran would have a field day if things were to surface. So it was important to stay small, really small, which for Sami translated into not much more than a dog-eared map of New York City and five hundred dollars in real twenty-dollar bills.

One of the Libyans had been on his tail since Brooklyn, a pockmarked, shark-faced man who had shown up on the third day in a yellow cab and hadn't said so much as hello to Sami ever since.

It took some backpedaling in the perfume section of Bloomingdale's on 60th Street and Lexington to finally get rid of his man. The fellow was no good at it anyway, though Sami had to give him time to make it look natural. After finally ditching the Arab, he continued to roam around just as he'd been doing for the past few days. His three-day lockup had confused things a little. The Colonel had given him six locations to cover on different days of the week. His contact could appear at two of those locations on a set day at five and six in the afternoon. One day's grace period had been added to account for any hitches when he arrived. But not three days. It was just the sort of plan that sounded okay on paper but turned out to be full of holes when it came time to act on it. This wasn't because the planners at the Office were inept; they just had a chronic problem underestimating their unwitting adversaries: the folks at State Security, especially Section Nineteen in Tehran.

So Sami had started his rounds on the fourth day, allowing the pockmarked Libyan to stay behind him while he wormed his way through long stretches of the island going north and south. He hadn't really counted on being followed at first but figured that if they were to tail him, there would always be time to spot his Office contact at the initial meeting place of the day, then proceed to lose the tail, and catch up with the contact at the second location.

All the while he'd had to fight to stay focused, to keep himself from being spellbound by the city, pushing his way through the dense afternoon rush of pedestrians around midtown Manhattan, to arrive at an appointed location to see no one there. Only this morning he had finally gotten anxious enough to take a chance with Damadi from Section Nineteen. But Damadi had given him little except for a bogus-sounding story about some Pakistani gadget man, who was more likely than not nonexistent.

This left Sami with one more set of five and six o'clock walk-bys and nothing further. In time he made his way down Broadway back to the garment district. At the foot of the statue of the old Jewish tailor on 38th and Broadway a mother and her two daughters sat eating slices of a fuzzy-looking orange-colored fruit Sami had never seen before. No sign of his contact. He zigzagged slowly, going further west. On 40th Street and Ninth Avenue he saw two homeless men who had found a beat-up child's kite in the Dumpster and were attempting to make the thing fly. Watching them as he passed, Sami imagined an alternate life where he was one of those kite-flying, shopping cart–rolling, garbage-scavenging, noisy neglected Americans who had never been made to find the proper translation for an Intel compound word like a *dead drop*. The moment passed and soon he was walking by his second contact point, the AfterBurner bar on Ninth Avenue and 48th Street, where no one was waiting for him and his watch said six o'clock.

Maybe no one was meant to have come. Maybe the Colonel was baiting him for bigger stakes, though he couldn't see to what purpose. He found himself drawn inside the bar. A considerable move, since never before had he done anything like this. He was a thirty-year-old man who had never sat inside of a bar, never ordered a drink from a barman or -woman, never known the self-perpetuating melancholy of a bar jukebox except through the books he had read and the scenes he had imagined through them while pounding the pavements in the streets of London and Paris. In Tehran none of this would have mattered, of course, since in Tehran there were no bars to enter, no drinks to order. Manhood was gauged under a different light over there and you were probably better off not yearning for out-of-reach details.

He wedged himself between a thin old black man who was pleasantly drunk, crooning to himself, and a heavyset middle-aged woman with a bottle of beer and a shot glass in front of her. The bar stools were red, the tables in the back were red, the wall was red, even the faces of the tired customers were red. There was a general redness to this place that in the muted light was oddly appealing to Sami. He ordered a Guinness because it sounded familiar. The woman sitting next to him turned to stare and rub her eyes. A younger crowd of college kids came in, laughing their way to the back of the bar. He overheard a pony-tailed man two seats to his left shout something to someone about the "beauty of those helical magazines," and how it was too bad that they were outlawed.

His beer was as bitter as death but he drank it anyway. The

woman next to him, who was still rubbing her eyes, told him, "Guinness makes me gag."

"What do you suggest I drink, then?" he asked politely. He really wanted to know. Somebody had put change in the jukebox, a mournful love song.

"Their vodka is only Gordon's here. It's watered down but the shot's healthy." She winked.

By the time Sami was on his third shot of Gordon's, Joanna had told him her address and that she was in the middle of writing a cookbook that had alternating chapters on sexual positions. The bar got hotter. Someone had selected an entire CD set of John Lee Hooker songs. Joanna's eyes were the only approachable part of her despite all the rubbing she administered to them. Sami ordered a fourth shot of vodka and a beer that he called Amstel rock twice until the sexagenarian bartender woman corrected him as she was setting the draft on the counter, "No, honey, it's bock, Amstel bock."

"This country is too big for me." It was a sigh and a whisper to himself more than anybody else, yet Joanna caught it.

"Where do you come from, Greece?"

He didn't know what to say to that. What was a Greek supposed to look like anyway? The one thing he kept going back to was his own lack of proper training and how he had been carrying it about like a dead weight these five, six years working for the Office. He ought not to be sitting in this bar right now. This was elementary but also probably beside the point. Since as far as the Americans went, if they had meant to have him picked up, they would have done so by now. So for the time being he was safe, he concluded a little too conveniently.

He ended up matching Joanna drink for drink. Soon the

old black man was dancing a twist with one of the college girls. Meanwhile Joanna appeared to levitate on her seat with each new round. And the two men who had been talking about helical magazines earlier were now joined by a third who took the black man's seat and began a discussion over "pre-ban magazines." Such arcane language, Sami was thinking, until the newcomer turned to him and asked, "What's your favorite pistol, buddy?"

Sami looked up and straight in front of him, noticing that the lady bartender had been replaced by another woman of about the same age. Then without giving it another thought he answered into his shot glass, "The old Browning Hi-Power. Best damn pistol ever made."

"Bullshit," came delightedly from two seats away. Another man asked, "Hey, where are you from? Never saw you here before."

"Me? I'm Alexander, the Macedonian," he mumbled before his mind started to fizzle.

He woke up with a fleeting headache and a solid thirst. A strong scent of cheap perfume pervaded the room. Disentangling himself from the mass of sheets and blankets he was under, he got up to search for water. He knew where he was and how they'd gotten here—a short taxi ride at the end of which Joanna had addressed the Indian cab driver as Mr. Sheik. He remembered up until their entering her dark studio. There had been no sex. Not that it mattered either way, but he still had an ineffable sense of being unclean for having put himself in Joanna's hands like this.

His fingers automatically searched for the leather pouch he'd strapped underneath his belt where he kept his money and the legit passport in his own name, Sami Amir. They were still there. Joanna didn't snore but made a high singsong whistling noise. He could hear the sound of cars over wet asphalt outside. Morning light was starting to seep in through the bathroom window and into the room. A round wooden table stood next to the opposite wall. He picked up a tall glass from there and automatically put it to his lips. Flat beer. He drank it distractedly anyway.

The stale alcohol made him want to retch. He'd had a sensation similar to this just about a year earlier watching a kid get the shit kicked out of him by some Revolutionary Guards thugs in Tehran. It had been an "exercise." At least that was what the Office liked to call it. Every now and then the Office would do a penetration of one of the city's policing organs, the Gendarmerie, the Basij, or the Revolutionary Guards. They would know what a certain squad was up to on a certain evening and they would choose to "install" themselves in the middle of an op. "It will keep you on your toes" was the stock official explanation for such exercises. On this particular night Sami and three other men had instructions to catch up with a Revolutionary Guards roundup detail before one of the freeway exits and join them in whatever they were doing. It was the sort of useless, dirty job that made you hope for foreign assignments. The other three guys from the Office, being with the "Domestic Department," had plenty of experience with this sort of thing. In truth they were something of a different breed from the likes of Sami. They could talk the talk and walk the walk of the Basij crowd and the Revolutionary Guards. They'd been chosen for the job not only because they were smart but also because they were bullies at heart. Someone like Sami would never have been picked up by the Colonel had it not been for his facility with a useful foreign language, added to the convenience of his not having any blood attachments to anyone.

The pretense that night was to act the part of a secondary Guards backup team. When Sami and his associates had come to the appointed place, the real Guards soldiers already had a group of kids out of their cars and against the wall. One of the victims, a boy of about seventeen, was curled up on the ground, in a fetal position, bleeding from the mouth. The soldiers, five of them, took turns smacking the kid's face with the butts of their rifles while one of them stood watching over the other kids. "This is the only mama's boy who's been drinking alcohol. His mouth smells like a toilet," one of the soldiers said. Then the circle widened to allow Sami's group to get some hits in. When Sami's turn had come up he'd kicked the kid in the rear just to have contributed something.

But the next day he'd gone screaming to the Colonel, "I'm not going to be a part of any more Internal Exercises. Why don't you send me abroad?"

And what was it the Colonel had said then?

"We're not in this business to see that justice is done," the man had barked, without letting himself get distracted from cleaning out his pipe bowl.

Perhaps even now it was really the Colonel he couldn't get out of his mind. The Colonel, that pipe-smoking Middle Eastern spymaster who had saved Sami from the horrible boredom of army life by detouring him into the Office instead; that odd entity entrenched deep in the bowels of the Islamic Republic's power source, with his immense collection of classical CDs and a closet full of colorful ties that he never wore.

During that slight confrontation of last year the purity of

the Colonel's statement had rocked Sami in a pretty nasty way, not because he thought the answer itself was so monstrous but because of how downright honest it was. Today Sami had his highly sought-after foreign posting and he'd already managed to get himself drunk in a Manhattan bar. He recalled again that luckless kid the Revolutionary Guards soldiers had beaten up for drinking alcohol. Freedom sounded like an overblown word from this vantage point—here where you had the luxury to drink yourself to death like Joanna on that bed, Joanna who snored like a medieval flute and who had been on her way downhill since the beginning of time.

A full twenty dollars remained on the phone card Sami had bought on his arrival at the airport. He knew he ought put his clothes on, walk a few blocks, and make the call to London on a public phone. Instead he found himself sitting on Joanna's toilet seat and twisting the cheap Korean encryption device over the receiver.

A tinny, almost robotlike voice answered on the other end, "Daryush speaking."

The primary signal for London was supposed to come with pre- and post-Islamic names. If whoever was taking the call came out with a name, any name, that was not Islamic, it meant there was trouble. It took a few seconds for Sami to let that sink in. He'd never thought about what he'd say if the trouble signal was actually given.

Finally he identified himself and asked to speak with Mohsen, the Colonel's code for overseas communications.

"You know that is not possible right now," the robotic voice answered.

Then there was a pause that lasted at least five excruciating seconds. Sitting on Joanna's toilet on this side of the Atlantic

Ocean, Sami could almost feel the other man thinking this one through. Trouble could mean a lot of things, including a turned emissary with a barrel of a gun to his head right now. How could the other man be sure if Sami was not turned? And if he wasn't, then shouldn't he have known better than to ask for Mohsen in London at a time like this?

"Look, can't you put me on a three way?"

"That's a negative."

"What's the problem?"

"You are on your own." Then, as an afterthought, the voice added, "Like me."

That could have meant anything. Sami still waited. There was a high-pitched clearing of a throat, and then, "More than that I can't tell you right now. Mohsen wants to know if there's progress."

He felt as if this conversation was taking place in a room full of ether. The two of them had to speak over each other's heads in order to reach some rarefied form of understanding.

"Progress on whose part?" Sami asked. "Us or the Backgammon players?" Backgammon being Section Nineteen.

The man offered him another silence. He saw that the light had gone on in the room. Joanna was sitting up in bed smoking a cigarette.

"Listen, I've got to go. Tell Mohsen the offering is a bunch of Lemons from North Africa. All amateurs except one." He thought for a little bit and then added without bothering to talk in code, "Nineteen has their man, too. He's expendable. Either that or he doesn't have enough clearance to realize he's expendable. Tell Mohsen the whole thing reeks of a setup job. There's a phony story about a gadget man. But have them check on it anyway. Nur is the name. Check that with our friends in the southeast, too. By the way, my connection was not here. What's going on?" He didn't wait for an answer to that one and quickly hung up.

"Are you happy, mister?" Joanna looked bloated and lost. She wore a white nightgown and her substantial calves stuck out from under the blanket.

"Only when I'm on offshore leave."

"Are you a sailor?"

Sami nodded. He imagined Joanna as a giant Mickey Mouse. Khosravi in the Printing Department had somehow found out that Sami was off to America and had asked for a Mickey Mouse for his eight-year-old daughter.

"Are you going to leave me now? You're not a cop, are you? What's your name anyway?"

"Sami."

"Is that a Jewish name? You don't have to run, I'm not going to attack you. I brought you home with me because you looked as bad as I feel. And that's pretty bad. When a man offers to buy rounds for half the people sitting at the bar, you know he's in trouble."

"Is that what I did?"

"Just about."

It seemed as if Joanna was offering him shelter with no strings attached, Joanna being the ultimate dream of half the penniless young men around the world desperately trying to get to America. Here was a familiar story: he could shack up with Joanna right now and no one would know the difference. Get married, get himself a green card, then take off for California on his own and leave yet another lonely American woman knocking on love's door.

"Hey, do I seem repulsive to you?"

Her manner of asking was so matter-of-fact that she might have been talking about a third party in the room.

"You don't have to be," he said.

He was standing by the kitchen window looking down on Eleventh Avenue. A black Lincoln was parked across the street, its windows tinted. There were thousands of cars like that in the city, with no distinguishing marks to tell one apart from the other. But he was sure he'd seen this one before. Where? During a glimmer of lucidity while stumbling out of the AfterBurner bar last night? Or even earlier, earlier than yesterday, perhaps as the car was hanging back outside of a Duane Reade pharmacy on Eighth Avenue two days ago when he'd gone in to buy himself a Snickers bar?

Was this the reason he was being left in the dark for now? Had the Office contact picked up the tail they had on him and decided to walk away for the time being? But he couldn't really see the Arabs chasing him around the city in a black Lincoln, even if they did have plenty of limousine service chauffeurs among them. Except for that fat Libyan, the guys he'd seen in the Brooklyn house were your ordinary immigrant working mules before they were Moslem revolutionaries. You only had to look at their faces to see that. Then what about Damadi from Section Nineteen? No again. This sort of thing was out of Damadi's range. That man was a greengrocer at heart, a traveling salesman who cared more about his rugs and his silverware than anything else. God knew which cleric's daughter he'd taken for a wife back in Tehran so he could get the New York posting. And now that he had what he wanted he wasn't going to risk his lucrative export business by getting his hands dirty through anything so chancy as meddling in unnecessarily risky stuff.

When Sami turned around he saw that Joanna was standing next to him. Her cigarette breath was dizzying. He was truly captivated by her ugliness, the deep furrows in that tired flabby face, the smudged lipstick that might have been forgiven on a girl forty years younger, and those puffy fingers that had held on to so many bottles of cheap American beer through the years.

At least in Tehran the playing field was a little more level for these unlovely women of the world. They had the luxury of hiding behind the shadows of their own veils and saving the real damage for more private realms. Had his own mother been alive, she would have been around Joanna's age, the American mother he had never seen. Had she been beautiful at least? The legacy she had left him was one of not belonging. He was a half-American who worked for a secret cell of the Iranian government that even its own intelligence service knew nothing about, and an Iranian whom everyone "back home" mistook for a foreigner, an American.

He was tired. He looked past Joanna at a calendar on the kitchen wall that was way out of date.

She followed his gaze. "Oh that. That's nothing, it's from three years ago actually, when I was trying to lose some weight."

The black Lincoln wasn't going anywhere, Sami noted.

"You look troubled, son. I promise I won't molest you," she laughed. "Let me give you a massage."

He looked at her.

"I'm really pretty good at it, you know."

Joanna had curiously deft hands. Lying on her bed with his shirt off and his face sunk into her pillow while she massaged his back, Sami thought back on the Moslem "freedom fighters" in Brooklyn. What would they say if they saw this? Would they damn the half-American to eternal hellfire for drunkenness? For allowing his flesh to be rubbed and kneaded by a stranger, this infidel woman's powerful arms?

3

THE BUILDING, SO REMOVED as to almost border the Williamsburg naval yards, seemed like a strange retreat for Brooklyn's Moslem militant elite. While they waited out on the street the men stood out like sore thumbs. Most of them were brawny, bearded Middle Easterners dressed in army surplus fatigues and kaffiyehs. The time was one o'clock on a Friday afternoon and the scene an open invitation for the positively nervous NYPD/FBI Anti-terrorism Task Force to come nosing around.

Back in Tehran the Office had paid an Egyptian stool pigeon to bring them up to date on what some clever analyst from an open-source American intelligence newsletter had first dubbed the Jersey City/Brooklyn Mosque Connection. The Office already knew that the stoolie was feeding the same information to Egyptian intelligence, and possibly the FBI as well. But as long the fellow believed his goods were being paid for by the *legitimate* Iranian security apparatus and not the Office itself, it didn't matter who else he sold it to.

It was information you could get from other sources anyway. A lot of people already knew about the nasty split between the so-called extremists and the others at Brooklyn's Abu Bakr mosque in the wake of the World Trade Center bombing. Bad blood was brewing among the "brotherhood." Some American Moslems openly accused the blind Sheik Omar of the now infamous Shalabi assassination in Brooklyn. Others spoke of back stabbers among the faithful and threatened revenge for what was called the Emad Salem debacle, named for the Egyptian informant who had helped the FBI trap the same Siddig Ali gang that had been planning to blow up just about every other major landmark around New York City not too long ago.

This was all serious stuff, but also more than a little confusing for anyone but the die-hard student of fashionable terrorism in general and Islamic terrorism in particular. Life went on, in other words. Fresh news replaced yesterday's headlines. The average New Yorker had no idea who Siddig Ali was or why Shalabi had been assassinated by his own people. The name of Emad Salem might sound to the American ear like a corruption of the tongue. The blind Sheik Omar was a vaguely familiar sight thanks to a few newspaper stories and television images. But for how long? How many people would really know just how close Siddig Ali and his hopelessly inept gang of bombs-for-hobby terrorists had come to effecting their inconceivable Manhattan nightmare? Worse still, how many people would know or remember that the FBI had had an informant, the same Emad Salem, who had warned them of an impending catastrophe *before* the World Trade Center bombing had occurred?

The answer to all these questions was, not many. Not many people at all, except for those whose job it was to follow this deadly sport from a distance and up close. In the Middle East a number of intelligence agencies were interested parties from quietly opposing sides of the field. But only in Iran, where the tug-of-war between the moderates and the America haters was so acute, were the stakes as high. A major act of terrorism on American soil with Iranian hands behind it could be a godsend to the America haters in Tehran. It would bring Yankee wrath back into the Persian Gulf and force the moderates to retreat from the political picture altogether. Which was why something like the Jersey City/Brooklyn Mosque Connection gave major ulcers to Sami's bosses back at the Office. They were forever scratching their chins trying to come up with preventive measures to make sure America was not rocked a second time by some out-of-control Middle Eastern crew, and they *especially* didn't want any Iranian hand behind the so-called Mosque Connection.

So on the surface the task that the Office had given Sami appeared cut and dried. He had to get to the bottom of whatever was being planned in New York by the America-hating zealots back home and nip it in the bud. Once the Office had gotten word that Section Nineteen of State Security was planning the unthinkable with Arab hands—to go for another major landmark on American soil—they'd pushed for their only truly fluent English speaker, Sami, to infiltrate Nineteen with a hope and a prayer that the section head would recognize the value of sending an "American" over for the New York job. So far, so good, because that was exactly what had happened.

But in the end, what was Sami supposed to do when he hooked up with Section Nineteen's Libyans in Brooklyn? How was he to put a stop to Nineteen's mad scheme without actually playing the role of a snitch to the Americans or killing the Arabs? And if that second option was on the agenda, then why hadn't the Colonel come out and told him so?

Outside of the warehouse he casually glanced around the outlying blocks for signs of surveillance. At least thirty men stood in small groups waiting to go inside for the Friday prayer sermon. They were mostly Arabs, a few Pakistanis, a tall black man wearing dark sunglasses who might have been an American, and three Afghans. He naturally gravitated toward the Afghans because he heard them speaking a Persian dialect, but then thought better of it. Surveillance was beside the point. The secluded location was a clever stroke. You figured the Bureau people (already in jitters over how thoroughly they'd screwed up on the World Trade Center bombing, when they hadn't paid attention to their own hired informant's warnings) would have the entire New York City Moslem community under some sort of surveillance. You'd be watched on either side of the river. A quiet location like this afforded room to watch your watchers.

The fat Libyan who had conducted Sami's interrogation earlier stepped away from a circle of Arabs and came toward him.

"I've been a bad host not spending more time with you the past week," he said with obvious lack of sincerity. There was a mocking tone to his voice that Sami had found disturbing since that first day, as if the two of them should be privy to some sort of understanding that excluded everybody else.

An NYPD car slowly turned from the other end of the

street. Besides the cop car and the men waiting to go inside the improvised mosque, there was no one else on the block.

"So what is it they call you around here?" Sami asked, keeping his eyes on the blue vehicle passing them by.

"Musavi. Pleasure is all mine, friend."

Fat Musavi made an air-embracing gesture with his hands that called for reciprocation. In the meantime other men were starting to look Sami over. Besides the Libyans, whom he'd met along with Musavi, the rest of these people were strangers to him. Bilal, the tail he'd left behind at Bloomingdale's earlier in the week, had just dropped him off here in his yellow cab and driven away without saying one word. By now Sami wasn't sure which made him more uncomfortable: the police car or the warehouse? Or Musavi?

Turning to the Libyan, he said, "Do you think it's very smart of them to show their hands so plainly?" He meant the NYPD.

"They know better than to try anything. There would be war on this street before they got into our *masjid* here."

The booming voice of the black man wearing sunglasses answered his question. Both Sami and Musavi turned their attention to him. The man was an American, after all, and on the taller side of six and a half feet. He wouldn't take his eyes off Sami and his statement on making war had been delivered as if it were being handed to an NYPD snitch. The moment was tense and awkward.

Musavi finally broke it by introducing Sami as "Brother Jamal out of California. I personally vouch for him."

"California, hey?" The tall black man nodded to the agreed-upon identity. "Abdul-Karim from right here in Brooklyn. *Salaam aleikum*, brother."

Sami gave the customary *W'aleikum salaam*, which seemed to pacify the big fellow for the time being. The latter then retreated to the inside of the building and began frisking the worshipers one by one as they went inside. It was a necessity to which all the men submitted with determined resignation, as if this, too, was a part of their faith—the willingness to go through the humiliation of being searched before entering a house of worship.

When everyone, including Sami, had gone through the door and been searched by Abdul-Karim, one of the Arabs stepped up and did the same thing to the American. The whole spectacle seemed a little strange. Stranger still was the space the men had entered. The building was two stories high, the bottom floor about a basketball court long with a fairly tall ceiling and nothing in it except some old meat hooks on a rolling belt that no one had gotten around to taking off. The floor was cheaply carpeted except for the area near the pulpit, where a more expensive-looking rug had been laid. The men took off their shoes at once and made a half circle in the middle of the room. One of the Arabs went up to the pulpit and without ceremony started rattling in Arabic. There was a moment of quiet when he seemed to have run out of breath and then all of a sudden his listeners, as if on cue, shouted a great *Allah Akbar*. This provoked the speaker to hurry his next batch of words even more, followed by cries of *Allah Akbar* from all around, and then a tumult of voices and shouts and God Is Greats, coming on the heels of one another.

Sami stood there with his mouth hanging open. He'd seen some strange acts of devotion in his time. He'd seen grown men cut their own heads open with naked swords for the glory of God, he'd seen the frenzied weeping of multitudes around a fallen Shiite saint's mausoleum, he'd seen angry and restless devotion with all the cruelties these things could entail. What he hadn't figured on, however, was coming to America to witness a sort of zealous rage that was automatic. These men seemed to be following a formulaic script, as if convinced that invisible cameras were recording their every move for a higher authority.

"You come this way, Brother Jamal," Musavi whispered into Sami's ear.

He followed Musavi and the American Abdul-Karim up a flight of steps to a wide corridor that rounded the upper floor until they came to a space directly above the man downstairs giving the sermon. The ground around one of the beams rising from the lower floor had been dug out in places so that one could get glimpses of the congregation below. It was also an ideal defense in case the place should ever come under siege from the police. Voices from underneath funneled right through these cracks and made ringing echoes on the empty upper level.

Hazrat, whom Sami still hadn't figured to be an Arab or an American, was sitting on a small prayer rug in the middle of the room. He got up to embrace Musavi. Then all the men, including Sami and Abdul-Karim, sat down on the floor.

One of the three Libyans who had driven with Sami from the airport on that first day was standing near the window looking out. He kept up a sustained tapping of his fingernails over the glass, probably to deflect the pickup of any remote recording device. His name was Abdullah, an all-purpose nobody whose function was simply to be there at other people's beck and call. Short and squat, with a jet black beard so thick as to form a sizable round ball around his face, he stared out into the world with determined incomprehension—a blank slate and a fortunate martyr in his own eyes. At the Brooklyn house Sami had noticed that Abdullah often served as a punching bag for another Libyan who was a devoted *Soldier of Fortune* reader and a karate buff. Right now this other Libyan was standing guard over the stairway leading to the second floor.

Sami still couldn't put a fix on any of these guys. Were they Section Nineteen freelancers or did they belong to Musavi and Libyan Intel after all? Only Damadi could have answered that question for him, but by asking it he knew he would be dropping his disinterested mask for the Section Nineteen resident in New York. That wouldn't be smart. The fraud of hierarchy had to be preserved at all costs. And for now, at least, Sami had to show that he couldn't care less if his confederates were out of work Spetsnaz specialists or chimpanzees from the local zoo.

With everyone seated, the man Sami called Hazrat pulled out an oversized notepad and pen from a sack and started to scribble something in Arabic for Musavi's benefit. For a second the noise from below died down and they heard footsteps coming up the stairs. Sami, Abdul-Karim, Hazrat, and Musavi turned to look. The Libyan guard at the stairway had moved back to let the newcomer up. For a minute Sami was thinking this must be the fabled gadget man, Nur, whom Damadi from Section Nineteen had talked about. But as soon as the man's head appeared above the railing Sami could tell this was no Pakistani. He had all the features of a small Levantine Arab, maybe Lebanese or Palestinian. He looked intelligent and paranoid and he created an acute feeling of discomfort as soon as he walked into the room. He sat down without making any particular greeting to anyone and immediately launched into a tirade about their choice of a meeting place.

"Look, when I agreed to this I knew I was taking a big risk. But that doesn't mean we have to take *unnecessary* risks, all right?"

Hazrat quickly interjected something in Arabic. Sami knew barely enough Arabic to understand he'd just said they should only speak Arabic here. This explained the question of Hazrat's nationality.

"But there are those of us here who cannot speak the language," Abdul-Karim put in. "How can we discuss anything if we can't understand one another, brothers?"

"Then we'll write everything down," Hazrat continued.

Musavi added, "How can we be sure this place hasn't been bugged?"

The newcomer shook his head. His English was native with a slight hint of a very old accent. "Then why are we here? Why choose a place that you know is going to be under their eyes?"

All heads turned to Abdul-Karim.

He smiled. "Brothers, this is the best that could be done under the circumstances. There's a lot of tension in the city nowadays. You can't turn around and build yourself a *masjid* without stepping on another brother's toes. Besides, this was the clearest way to find out who is with us and who isn't."

"What does that mean?" Sami asked him.

"Shhh!"

While they had been talking, the voices from down below had reached a crescendo so that everything they said was drowned out in a cacophony of other voices. Now there was a temporary lull downstairs so that they all had to maintain a brief silence until the worshipers started up again. The scene was so absurd that Sami would have been tempted to laugh, if he hadn't recalled that it was precisely a gang of amateurish bombers like these that had nearly succeeded in bringing down one of the tallest buildings in the world.

Abdul-Karim leaned into Sami's ear and whispered, "Forgive me, friend, that man who has just joined us—his name is Zuheir. He is a biochemist here. He can provide us with certain . . . chemicals."

Zuheir looked back and forth from Sami to Abdul-Karim. His nervousness had begun to rub everyone the wrong way. Hazrat was twisting his prayer beads in his right hand and muttering to himself. Musavi, on the other hand, looked alert and sharp-eyed. And it didn't escape Sami that the main object of Musavi's attention was Sami himself.

Musavi spoke. "There are some things, my brothers, that may be done only under—how it is said?—under very rigorous standards. We had to measure each man's willingness and also each man's . . . how you say it? Nerves."

"Is that why you had me followed around last few days?" Sami cut in.

Musavi smiled. He was about to continue, but this time he was cut off by the biochemist Zuheir, who seemed to have suddenly remembered something. "Who are all those men downstairs? Why are *they* here?"

"I assure you they are fellow brothers, but they know nothing. It is Friday and they are here to pray," Abdul-Karim explained. Then he took the notepad from in front of Hazrat and wrote, "Now we will all leave here. There's a van outside. We will get in. We will drive somewhere and discuss what we have to discuss."

There was no protest this time. On the ground floor the worshipers had finished listening to the sermon and were preparing to begin the Friday prayer. No one paid much attention to the men who had just descended the stairs. The place smelled of male energy and male bodies, and in that, at least, it didn't differ much from a regular mosque in the Middle East.

4

TO A TRANSLATOR like Sami, who for a long time now had had to weigh ideas word by word, it was obvious why a map could never be the territory. Having been the Office's unofficial wordsmith, he was more aware than most other men that words like *spy* and *spying* carried a set of different connotations from one country to another. Back in 1980, for example, when the American embassy in Tehran had fallen to the mob, the looters had come to call the place the Den of Spies. To call it that was their grandest gesture of antipathy for the trade. Sami had learned that the reason why a Middle Easterner could never attach fanciful associations to the craft was because he would automatically think of spying as domestic surveillance—screwing your own people, electric shocks and hot iron bars, dingy rat-infested cells where a fat slob with angry bloodshot eyes would threaten to stick his penis in your little sister's behind if you didn't talk.

Maybe this was why even at the Office no one ever referred to spying as such. Intelligence was another no-word. Little was said except for the agreed on pretense that theirs was the only true direction. *Somebody* had to stand in the way of those bearded Koran-toting messengers of God from across town, right? Stand in the way of Section Nineteen and the men who bankrolled its agendas.

All of which had brought Sami to here and now, sitting in the basement of a small falafel joint in the heart of Greenwich Village in Manhattan with three other men—an American, a Libyan, and another American of Lebanese descent—who were speaking of infidels and body counts the way other men might speak of good books and great basketball dunks. Plotting destruction was so abominably easy! Sami wondered if all those fresh faces he'd seen on the street above them—the college kids and the street musicians and the hipsters and the cappuccino-sipping tourists in the cafés off Macdougal Street . . . the leather-clad, ponytailed, earring-in-one-ear tough guys and their admirers—he wondered if any of these people had any idea just how perfectly they represented everything the men in the basement of the falafel place wished to annihilate.

"The point of the matter is you don't have to go high tech for what you're proposing," the chain-smoking Zuheir was saying.

"The man has a point," Abdul-Karim put in.

They were sitting around a wooden table with a clear plastic cover. A single weak lamp hung from overhead and the four corners of the room were stacked with supplies. Except for the almost absurd nature of their dialogue, you would have thought these men were getting ready to deal for an all-night card game. It was cold and damp and for the first time in New York Sami got a feel for just how cold winter could get in these parts. He didn't like it, didn't like being here, and wouldn't know *how* to do what he had to do even if someone had hit him over the head with it.

Earlier, behind the wheel of the gray van they'd driven in, Abdul-Karim had worked at shaking off any tails they might have following them over the bridge. Sami hadn't spotted the black Lincoln today and decided to keep quiet about it for the time being. They'd driven to a Bangladeshi lunch stop frequented by cab drivers on Ninth Avenue and there were greeted by a jolly subcontinental proprietor who had immediately guided them through the back door to a side street. From there it was across to an entrance of the Port Authority through which they'd rushed over to the Eighth Avenue side. Next a taxi ride to Washington Square Park and then on foot to the falafel place. It was a roundabout way of doing things, but at least it showed *these* cabbies-turned-terrorists were serious about whatever it was they wanted to do. Now someone had to break the ice.

Musavi picked up the thread of the argument that had begun to develop. "My government would like to know why it is that yours"—cocking his head at Sami—"wishes to engage in this business?"

Sami offered a low grunt that was meant to indicate cynicism or lack of respect on his part for the other man and his so-called government. Musavi was trying to draw him out. He didn't know why, but by now he knew that at least none of the other men were aware of this. Musavi was the only real player here, while these other guys were extras—probably clueless ones at that. So the only appropriate response *was* the grunt, as if to say, "I acknowledge your game but do not trust you well enough to play along just yet."

Zuheir wanted to get back to the main topic.

"But the main issue here," Abdul-Karim started to say, "is more than a couple of blasts, brother. I, too, would like to know what is at stake for Brother Jamal from California." He winked, grinning at the continuation of the Brother Jamal out of California joke.

"I do what my superiors ask of me," Sami said. "I don't question their motives. I think, but only so far as it concerns the job I'm given to do. No more, no less. I thought all this should be clear to you men."

"That's a beautiful answer"—Musavi grinned—"it is very professional."

"But what *is* your job?" Zuheir asked him now.

"We will provide."

"Can you get us blasting caps?"

Sami gave the man a noncommittal look. "I'm good at lending and borrowing."

"What does that mean?" Zuheir pressed on.

"It means his people are generous," Musavi said. "And I have a man upstate who has a hundred pounds of C-4 from Canada ready for delivery."

"Nonsense."

"Why nonsense?"

Sami had retreated momentarily, letting them play their hands out to one another. It seemed to him these were the sort of men who would crack at the news of treachery precisely because they'd been worried about it for so long. A halfway decent New York City detective or a U.S. attorney could have a field day with someone like Zuheir.

"What do you know about C-4?"

"It's clean, it's available, and our money man has arrived."

"What about this fellow Nur?" Sami asked.

Musavi answered, "Nur is on his way. There is no game until we have the material. And I do have the material."

"I have a tough time believing the Libyan government would return a whole hundred pounds of the stuff it took so much effort and money to smuggle out of the United States."

Sami had thrown this out as a sign that he was busy thinking, that he wasn't sure about the fellow brothers around this table. Then as he was saying it, it became clear to him that perhaps the only way to put an end to the troublesome Mosque Connection once and for all would be to instill an even deeper distrust for one another among the believers. The Americans and the FBI didn't understand these men just yet and perhaps they never would, not like they had understood their Russian opposites not so long ago. But if they weren't at least trying to make a pitch right about now, then they were fools. Utter fools.

"I have no idea what you mean," Musavi said acidly.

"Brothers . . ." Abdul-Karim had started to call for peace, but Sami didn't let him finish.

"All right, then, let's say I believe you, Brother Musavi. Question remains: which explosives dealer in North America in his right mind would sell a Libyan a single firecracker after Wilson?"

"What is Wilson?" Abdul-Karim and Zuheir asked together.

"Ex-CIA who got too chummy with the Libyans," Sami said.

There was a moment's silence. Musavi was looking hard at Sami. Finally he whispered hoarsely, "As they say here: let us cut the bullshit! You and I know the business, so how to get on with it?"

"That's better." Sami turned to the other two men. "All right, brothers, I think we can work together after all."

Musavi smiled.

Abdul-Karim shook his head and laughed to himself.

Zuheir looked from one man to the next askance. "What just happened here? I'd like to know. I still say fertilizer and fuel oil and blasting caps are enough for what we want to do."

"Man, what do you know about what we want to do, huh?"

Abdul-Karim's last words shut Zuheir up. Musavi and Sami looked at each other without saying another word. It was an ambience saturated with infantile promise, as if some cross-eyed painter had set out to paint a mosaic but instead created a distorted chess set.

5

THE OLD MAN was screaming Russian into the telephone. The row of ten public pay phones were attached to the back of the mini police station on 43rd Street where Broadway and Seventh Avenue diverged from one another. The time was still well before dusk but the scaffolding overhead made it seem much later. Sami waited. Slowly, the flashing signs and the neon from the north end of the square were starting to get tangled in his head with the voice of the old man at the pay phone repeating familiar Soviet Russian names: Stalin, Brezhnev, Andropov . . .

To Sami's and the old Russian's right, on the other side of Broadway, stood a huge billboard poster of a young man in an advertisement for a pair of jeans—taut, perfect stomach muscles rippling through three floors of office space being prepared for demolition.

Sami took in his surroundings. Times Square. Crossroads of the World. He was trying to recall the many times he'd seen a shot of these few city blocks through all the bootleg Hollywood movies he'd watched back home on video. It was a lonely feeling, this being here now. Maybe the only other time he'd felt quite as lonely was on a rainy night in London when he'd had to stay put at a Soho side street while "his charges," a pair of female-hungry Iranian Foreign Ministry nincompoops, were busy with a British whore two flights above.

It was pushing past 4:30 and the Russian showed no signs of letting up from that particular pay phone. Sami took two one-dollar bills from his pocket and laid them out on the ground directly in the old man's line of vision. After one more apparent round of Stalin bashing the Russian's eyes fell to the earth and immediately spotted the dollar bills. In a blink the old fellow was making haste for the money.

Even crazies, it seemed, had their normal moments. Sami put the receiver back on the phone and forced the encryption device over the speaker. Right away the telephone began to ring.

"Yahya."

"Is John."

"I've been ringing this number for ten minutes," the Colonel said. He sounded irritated.

Sami said, "Sorry, I thought this is another exercise: how to get somebody off the public phone who is mad at the Soviets."

"What?"

"Nothing. Where are you and how secure?"

"Don't worry, talk."

"First off, why am I here and what kind of a sham is this?"

"What's the problem?"

"Problem is you have a bunch of Arab cab drivers itching to become martyrs. I don't have to tell you they haven't a clue what they're up to. And the Bureau probably already has a few nice close-ups of every one of them, myself included, except I've been trying to blend in with the brothers."

"Stop right there. Back up."

"No, listen for a minute! I could leave New York on the next flight back and let the Arabs get themselves hung. They don't need our help for that. Believe me. The whole thing is like a bad joke."

"What about Nineteen?" The Colonel asked, dispensing with code.

"I can hint to their New York man it's all schoolboy stuff and pretend that as a Nineteen operative I won't stand for it. It would save us effort and keep Nineteen bogged down for a while trying to come up with something better."

"Who's their man? The Groom?" The Colonel asked, referring to Damadi's name in English as a direct translation of its original Persian.

"Yes. Except he's disappeared on me for now. Just plain disappeared. I'm telling you, something about all this doesn't sound right. Smells like a setup job."

There was silence on the line. He could imagine the Colonel chewing on the stem of his pipe while he tried to work through all this. What would an NSA cryptanalyst breaking in on this conversation possibly make of it?

"Look," Sami began again, "first off, you got some nonexistent Pakistani who is supposed to pop out of a box and work miracles."

"What makes the Pakistani nonexistent?"

"The fact that he's nonexistent."

He waited for the Colonel to answer that. But the other man remained silent, which only served to push Sami a little further toward the edge. The Colonel's silences were never uncalculated. Sami knew that. He also knew that the unspoken hint of yet another presence, i.e. the Pakistani specialist, changed the nature of the job altogether. It created the possibility of a genuine ticking clock, one that had to be located before shit happened. On a more personal note, it forced Sami to stay put.

He finally broke the silence himself. "You tell me, is he or is he not real, then?"

The Colonel answered, his voice sober. "We don't know yet."

Sami thought it through. If the Colonel was on the level—and there seemed no reason he shouldn't be—then this Nur character from Pakistan could only mean one thing: there had to be more than one puppet master inside the Mosque Connection web. For if Section Nineteen was actually controlling the fellow, then the Office, having already penetrated Nineteen, was bound to have a positive ID on him. Either that, or the Colonel was being ambiguous on purpose in order to keep Sami chained on this side of the Atlantic.

"You have more?" This time it was the Colonel who broke the long pause.

"I do. There's this fat Libyan who could be with their intelligence but comes across like a, like a . . ."

"Businessman?"

"Precisely." Sami was taken back. That was how he'd been thinking of Musavi all this time without exactly being able to put it into words.

"Listen, the *business* being lucrative these days, everyone wants to get in on the deal. Especially businessmen. Do you understand?"

"No need for philosophy now. What I need is direction."

"Bide your time. Play it their way."

"Like what? Drive a couple of hundred miles to buy new year putty. You know that sort of thing is nonsense."

"It might be. Then again it might not."

"What about this Nur?"

"We'll get back to you on that."

Sami thought aloud, "Why *their way*?"

"Because things are not looking too well around here."

The Colonel wasn't going to elaborate over the phone but Sami already knew exactly what he was talking about. This was supposed to be a secret, and yet within the ranks the men knew that the Office had already lost at least two good agents in the last month alone. Nineteen was leaning heavily on them, especially in Western Europe and Syria. If Sami came back right now, the other side might smell a rat and quickly figure out he'd been working for the Office all along. On top of all that, the elections were coming up in Tehran and Nineteen was nervous as hell about not being able to effect an international incident that might help settle their own candidates in the cabinet and the parliament.

He started to ask what had happened to his contact in New York City. But the line had already gone dead. He could almost feel the slam of the receiver on the other side, probably the Colonel's incipient anger with himself for hinting too freely. Or else a carefully chosen moment of that to demonstrate sincerity. In the meantime Sami was already well aware that all the Colonel had really said was to say absolutely nothing. What exactly did it mean to play it their way?

He looked up and around him. In a brightly lit restaurant on the west side of Broadway the waiters and waitresses were dressed in World War II military uniforms. Out on the sidewalk a man was petting a huge yellow snake wrapped around his shoulders. Everywhere there were cinemas, theaters, pizza shops, novelty stores. Even an unlikely cast of black men decked out in space costumes reading from the Bible and shouting hellfire at their mostly white audience.

Suddenly he knew why he had never wanted to be a part of this other world. He needed order, not chaos. The order of old Father O'Malley's missionary school in Tehran. Waking up to neatly spelled-out chores. Getting a pat on the back for doing a good job and avoiding all the things he was supposed to avoid. Uncertainty was rough waters; uncertainty was New York City; it was America.

6

THE NEXT MORNING he woke up to the unmistakable sound of a nine-millimeter being cocked. It was still dark out, and the only thing he could see was a shadow standing a few feet away from him. He thought, This is it, Sami, just remain still and it will be over before it's begun. If they were to ask him what his last wish was right now, he'd tell them he only needed a couple of days to read a good book to its end in peace. No disturbances. No tasks to finish. No damned reports or translations to be handed to anyone—like that time back at the Caspian shore in Iran when he'd rented a bungalow near the beach and read the entire *Red and the Black* in seven sittings. He'd read it in Persian and in a bad translation at that. But who cared? The waves lapped to people's doorsteps at night; that's how high the water was . . . just a couple of carefree days by the sea with a good book . . .

"Brother Amir, are you ready?"

It was Musavi's voice. He had just come into the room and turned the light on. Now Sami saw that the gun was in the Libyan Abdullah's hand and he was trying to stuff it under his shirt. Musavi saw it, too, and there was a brief argument in Arabic until Abdullah finally gave up and handed the piece to the other man. Sami breathed a sigh of relief. A gun in Abdullah's hand was like a grenade without a fuse.

He stood up and looked sleepily back and forth from Musavi to Abdullah. The door was open and through it he could see Hazrat and Musavi's other Libyan sidekick praying the predawn prayer in the other room.

"Today is the day, my friend. We go and pick the stuff I promised."

"With what money?"

"I thought your people had money for us."

"Well, it will have to wait. There are some difficulties back home."

"Oh? I heard nothing from your countryman Damadi."

"That's because he hasn't been around to tell you anything. But I'm telling you: you put C-4 in the hands of these men," Sami pointed to Abdullah, who was walking out of the room, "they'll be rolling it in balls and sticking it in each other's ears."

"Is that the reason for the change with your people? Because you think we are not professional enough?"

"You can think that if you want. The fact is I can't supply you with enough money to cover a hundred pounds of C-4. Not now. Not any time soon."

"That is all right, the dealer says he can wait to get his money."

At that moment Sami was certain beyond a shadow of a doubt that Musavi's game had been a hoax from the very beginning. There are certain rules to every business. Two diamond merchants might trade a million dollars' worth of gems with no more than a handshake and a hug, but there was no way in hell that a black-market explosives dealer would wait for a nickel from anyone. Besides which, how was the fellow supposed to have known beforehand that his money wasn't being paid up front?

All this went through Sami's head in the time it took Musavi to make sure everyone was ready. Then Abdullah and Musavi started to talk hotly again in Arabic. He thought he knew what the trouble was: Abdullah wanted to do his morning prayer like everyone else while Musavi was telling him he could make it up later in the day. It was the sort of farcical scene a Hollywood film director would bet his career on. *Moslem extremists at work.* The evil Arab terrorist retreats to the cockpit to chant his stock Allah this and Allah that on his hands and knees before throwing the bullet-riddled body of a passenger off the airplane.

And yet . . . if this did happen to be what they'd all been waiting for, then Sami's choices seemed pretty clear cut. One option: Make an anonymous call to the FBI's New York office and tell them they had potential disaster on their hands. But what could the Bureau and American justice do to these people? Exactly nothing. There was zero material proof until they had the C-4 and there *was* no C-4. At this point Sami wouldn't have been surprised if Musavi promised them he could produce some Semtex from the delicatessen on the next block.

Then there was the more hands-on approach: Make a grab

for that semiautomatic Musavi had taken from Abdullah and shoot all four of the sons of bitches right there and then. He was sure this was the more preferable choice as far as the Office was concerned, since what the Office was really after was to inject dread into these people. And you certainly didn't have a very good chance of achieving that by bringing American law into the picture and having a couple of liberal New York Jewish lawyers take up the Arab cause for humanity's sake. No, the Colonel, Sami realized now, had wanted something much more drastic without actually saying it. And he hadn't said it because for Sami, as an infiltrator into Section Nineteen, there was no going back to Tehran if he killed these nitwits. Nineteen would hang him. Unless, and this was the big if, the Office had finally decided to play an endgame with not only Nineteen but the entire Iranian State Security setup, so that all the sides had chosen this moment to bring matters to a head before the elections in Tehran.

Either way he was in a tight spot, he thought to himself as they all piled into a van, especially with Nur still unaccounted for. His instructions had been left vague on purpose, no doubt as a form of insurance for the Colonel and the other fellow worthies. "Play it their way," the Colonel had said last night on the phone. And so he would, he'd go along with Musavi for the time being, to unearth Nur at least. Musavi himself might turn out to be nothing more than a small-time con man trying to dump a hundred pounds of barreled mud as C-4 explosive on Iranian intelligence. A suicidal act to be sure, and thus probably not the truth at all.

"I thought we were driving upstate?"

Musavi was pointing toward the bridge into Manhattan. "Do you really imagine, my Iranian brother, that our dealer friend could stand the anxiety of having a van full of Moslem men appearing at his doorstep upstate?"

"That's the smartest thing I've heard you say yet, Brother Musavi."

The van pulled up to a bus stop on Atlantic Avenue and Abdul-Karim got in. The *salaam aleikums* were passed back and forth like morning coffee.

"No sir," Musavi said, "the man will be meeting us right here in New York with the material. Saves us time and . . . how to say it? Risk."

No more words were exchanged until Musavi guided Abdullah to park the car by the same falafel joint in Greenwich Village where they'd talked shop on Friday. Zuheir the Lebanese chemical expert now got in the vehicle. No peace greetings this time. It was past 6:00 A.M. and still dark out.

Each man seemed distracted as the van rolled on. There was the towering Abdul-Karim, sitting across from Sami and looking almost blissful. Deep down he must have cherished the idea that today was his moment, that he had entered the faith's inner sanctum by finally connecting with some brothers from the Old World.

At one point Musavi had his two Libyans switch sides. Now the fan of *Soldier of Fortune* magazine and martial arts expert got behind the wheel. Sami heard the man's name for the first time, Ahmed. Ahmed drove the van to a public telephone booth on Bleecker Street. They waited. The phone rang twice, went dead, and then rang again twice more. Sami looked at his watch: 6:37. The van started moving again. Musavi guided the driver up Tenth Avenue now. It was Saturday and the streets were still empty. A left turn on 25th Street and the van slowed to a halt.

From the outside the place looked like an old municipal building. It had a dilapidated whitewashed facade and a tall arched window that covered the whole second floor. As the van backed up to park, the lights shone on the opposite side of the street revealing a sleeping pair of derelicts whose heads stuck out from the ends of their carefully folded pieces of cardboard. Ten yards to the left, on the same side of the street, was a window display of what looked to be a defunct garment warehouse, with mostly limbless mannequins making a humanlike chain across the display.

Musavi spoke: "I'll go in with Ahmed and Abdullah first. Then I'll come and get the rest of you."

"And why is that?" Sami asked him.

"I told you before, these Americans, they get nervous around too many of us."

"Go on ahead, brother," Abdul-Karim commanded.

The three Libyans up front got out the van and walked off. Now it was just Sami, the exceptionally quiet Zuheir, Hazrat, and Abdul-Karim.

"What about it?" Sami asked absentmindedly.

"What about what?" Abdul-Karim responded.

"You think art has a place in our lives?"

"I don't understand."

Zuheir shifted uncomfortably. Abdul-Karim and Hazrat looked at one another.

"I mean," Sami went on, "what about expressing yourself through a different medium? We could get a team together to go around this city and set off firecrackers with notes attached. You know what I mean? It could be our message to the world. A sublime message. Don't Mess with Us or Else."

"What does sublime mean?" Hazrat asked.

Zuheir became animated all of a sudden. "You Iranians are bullshit. Everything you say is shit. Big shit."

"No, we say small shit, too."

"Fuck you, Irani."

The F-word caused both Hazrat and Abdul-Karim to a utter a deep *Astaghfor-Allah*. After that everybody held his peace. Musavi and the other two had been gone for about five minutes. It was lighter outside and Sami could now see that some of the mannequins in the display window across the street had blood splattered patterns on their bodies. On top of the entrance somebody had spray-painted "Kami is an old queer." To think that somebody had gone to all that trouble to come here and spray-paint some oddity like that! The effort seemed as frivolous as sitting in a van on an early morning in New York so you could get your hands on fireworks that were going to kill and maim innocent human beings—two statements with varying degrees of extremity, that was all.

Musavi came back out. "Brothers, we are ready to do business."

Those were the last words Sami would hear for some time.

He woke up on sore knees hugging a very tall wooden post. A hideous bright light shone from up above into his face.

"Excedrin!"

He'd mumbled the word as if it were a charm. Excedrin painkillers had been his friend Mozart's great gift after one of his rare trips to America. Good old Mozart from the Western Europe Desk. One day Mozart had returned from an American assignment with half a suitcase full of those pills. Then before long the entire Office staff was popping them with alarming regularity. And four weeks later there was a black market for Excedrin all over the city.

Sami had to carefully raise both arms together up the post to be able to massage the area on his temple where the bump was. Somebody had handcuffed him to the beam. How long? He couldn't even begin to guess. No sign of the other men who had entered here with him. No windows either. He thought he saw a door opening but couldn't be sure. Above a certain height he just couldn't look up; the light was too bright. A tray of food. Somebody bending down. Not again! Maybe the Colonel had sent him to New York to get locked up by hospitable zealots who insisted on keeping him around.

"What about it?" he started. "Do I get to ask questions?"

He got a heavy-duty slap for that one. A stout hand giving it to him. On top of the bump on his face the slap hurt enough to make him want to cry. He pressed his eyelids together. The light seemed to have gotten twice as bright all of a sudden. His head was swimming. He saw a pair of shoes but no legs to go with them. Somebody was reciting from the Koran.

"Did I hear right?"

Another slap. Then the voice picked up from where it had paused. Something about God being angry for this and that. No more comments from Sami on this. He sorely needed some of that wonderful American Excedrin. The Koran recitation stopped and after a pause of ten or so seconds a voice in Persian asked, "What is your name?"

"Me?"

This time when the slap came he could taste the blood running from his nose. The voice asked his name again. But it didn't bother to wait for a reply. It went on. Why was he here? Who was supervising him? Aim, time, past, present . . . then long, nerve-racking pauses like they have on polygraph tests, pauses that will make the toughest men in the world wet their pants.

"Hey, I'm just a silly translator in the wrong place at the wrong time."

Half the questions came in English and half in Persian, so after a while it became a game for him to try and figure out what language was going to be next. Trick questions too: at least three times the voice, a different voice, asked a question in Hebrew. Russian as well. Even Arabic. They were trying to establish his identity. Once—already it seemed as if hours had passed—he blurted, "The pleasure is all mine," and immediately crouched to avoid the slap. But the slap never came. Half a dozen questions later, *thump!* He imagined it was late punishment for the cheek he'd shown before. Back and forth like that, while the light shone ever brighter. At some point he figured the voice wasn't live. It was a recording. Not that that put his tender mind any more at ease. The slaps after all were quite real.

He fell asleep. Or thought he had. Later he opened his eyes to see a man in a gray suite bending over him. "Do you know what this is?"

"An eagle?" It was a badge, a fake one.

The slap came from his blind side this time and he felt himself drifting. But somebody held ammonia under his nose and he started to gag.

"Name?"

"Sami Amir."

"Who do you work for?"

"Section Nineteen?"

"Is that a question?"

Now that was a trick question if anything. The fog of pain gave him enough room to take the question mark out of what he'd said: "Yes, I'm with Section Nineteen of Iranian State Security."

The slap came anyway.

"Oh, for the love of God," he said in Persian, ready for anything. But he didn't get hit this time. He felt like Pavlov's dog conditioned by a sadist.

"Do you know who I am?"

"I know who you're not."

The hand that had been tenderizing him from the blind side all this time now reached down from behind and unlocked his cuffs. This seemed like a step toward something bad. He'd keep quiet for a while.

The light shone brighter. An invitation to start talking.

"All right," he started, "you're not . . . let's put it this way, you're not any United States governmental organization with abbreviated letters—the ABC, the DEF, the FEG. I'm tired."

His interrogator muttered, "Good."

It so happened that oftentimes when you read a man's hand to him you were giving away your own.

"What other things am I not?" his interrogator asked.

There were a lot of things he might have been tempted to say had his wits been completely about him. For instance, he could have told them they were rushing it. Give me time and I'll come around. But obviously there *was* no time.

"I'll make it easy, friend: where's Musavi?"

The fellow in the gray suit stared at him for a while.

Sami became bold. "Just bring on that fuck Musavi."

The light dimmed. And now he could see that gray suit was an American, on the far side of fifty, with stringy gray hair slicked back. His eyes too were almost the color of his suit. He had a wide monkey mouth and shiny white teeth. There was a bead of sweat on his nose, a nose that had been broken at least once. The man who had been hitting him was an Arab. The type of heavy you'd consider breeding for your praetorian guards. He pulled up a table and three chairs and the American sat down.

"You think we're fucking around here?"

"Anything but."

"Why is the Iranian government sending agents this far?"

"I thought we were agreed we were going to start some fireworks."

"Don't bullshit me, asshole! Start from the beginning: how long have you been working for Nineteen?"

"Ten years."

At a sign from the American the Arab grabbed Sami's hair and yanked down until his nose was touching his crotch.

"Try again, boy," the American said. "How is it that a jerk-ball like you who's barely been in Nineteen for six months gets to be sent to New York City? You want to explain that one to me?"

"So you know!"

"That's not the question. What the hell does your security network have to gain by starting some half-assed operation in full view of American law enforcement. I want to know who really sent you. Why? And why now? Start!"

There was a pause.

"First off," Sami began, "tell your man here not to hit me anymore."

The American signed to the Arab, who backed off.

"Okay, where's Musavi?" Sami asked for the second time.

The American nodded to the Arab again. The other man walked over to the door and opened it. Musavi was there, bright and serious, a poster boy for corruption. He came over and took the other seat next to the American, looking intently at Sami.

"Mr. Amir," said Musavi, "how about taking a seat at our table so we can speak better."

Sami complied. "I assume those other three guys in the van with us, they're all . . ."

"Dead. Dead as doornails. Right now a New Jersey garbage truck is hauling their remains somewhere far from their loved ones. Now, I'd say you were in a lot of trouble, Mr. Amir. You've got a number of dead coconspirators who all have tight connections in the community. You've got a dead black Moslem whose people are not going to be pleased when they find out their brother is missing. And guess what? We could drop you off as a live bundle right out in front of the Atlantic Avenue mosque. You're aware, I suppose, that snitches have a very short life span in that community."

"How about yourself?"

"Me?" Musavi asked with fake alarm. "I'm another one of your missing friends as we speak right now. Arabs all over Brooklyn will be mourning the loss of Brother Musavi by tomorrow. That leaves only you, Mr. Amir."

"From the looks of things, I'd say you were in desperate need of friends," the American added.

"There's no need to threaten me. I'll start clean, and it goes something like this: just what is the point of you guys wanting this Mosque Connection finished? I don't know. But I'm willing to make an educated guess."

"Shoot," the American said.

"Bombing buildings Stateside is bad for business. Bad for everyone, almost. I came here to do the job you guys claim to have finished already."

"That still doesn't explain why Section Nineteen would send you here?"

"Because Security isn't happy with the way things are going back in Tehran."

"Don't get abstract."

"Nineteen wanted to supply these fools. Make the Americans nervous so they'd start throwing their weight around again in the Gulf. It's the surest way for those guys to stay in business—Nineteen, I mean. They'd like to get the Great Satan to bark so they can bark back. They are worried about losing the elections to the . . . liberals."

The American laughed. "Liberals?"

"Give us a break. We're trying."

Musavi broke his silence. "So who is it you really work for, then, Mr. Amir, if not State Security and Section Nineteen?"

Sami looked at the American. "Is it necessary to answer that?"

"Not as long as we're working on the same side. Are we working on the same side, Sami?"

Sami shrugged. "Hey, my job here is finished. Whom should I say I had the pleasure of meeting when I get back home?"

The American disregarded that question. "You seem to forget: Nineteen won't be very pleased at your performance if and when you get back. Does the name Zaheri ring a bell?"

"Of course, he's the head of Nineteen. This whole charade starts with him."

Musavi looked at the American and smiled. "I like a man who comes clean to us."

"And you think having gone to all this trouble to make things difficult here, Zaheri would be content to just give it up?"

"You seem to know more about that than I."

"Be careful, Amir, you're fishing again."

"Well, information is a two-way street, you see. I haven't a clue who you guys are."

The American got up from the table and Musavi followed suit. It was obvious the game was the American's. Musavi was his Middle Eastern jack-of-all-trades, his pimp and procurer.

"Eat your food, Sami boy. It's gonna get cold."

Sami looked over to the floor where the big Arab had set down a sandwich for him maybe hours ago. A cockroach was already having a go at the wrapping paper.

"How good are you with seven-digit numbers?"

"Depends on the number."

"You think you can handle 826-6585?"

Sami nodded. "I could use a gun."

Musavi laughed hard. "You bloody Iranians. You don't deserve the earth you occupy."

"Can I have a gun anyway?"

"Hey, Karim," the American shouted, "bring the man a gun. The whole thing, give him the whole thing."

Karim didn't seem at all pleased to be parting with the handy H&K and its state-of-the-art-looking suppressor. He set it down on the table in front of Sami and grunted. It was the sound of a not too bright individual burying his stillborn child.

"You never know who might want to hurt you, Sami boy," the American said.

"Right. Which leaves us with Nur. Is he real?"

Musavi and the American both turned to watch him. The American spoke. "A Baluchi by birth. CIA-trained during the Afghan war. Did a couple of independent stings inside Pakistan afterwards, which didn't make the Paks very happy. Last heard of he was in the Philippines. He set off a bomb in a crowded church and was thought to have gone up in smoke with it."

"Was he?"

"We don't know," Musavi said, "we were not there."

"To think I was trying to use you to get to him."

"If he's still alive, he'll pop up." the American said. "It's the old rumor-mill trick. Get all the parties nervous so they'll show their hands. Then he'll know who he wants on his side."

"And that doesn't make you nervous?"

"No," Musavi said. "But it should make *you* nervous, Mr. Amir. I'm dead, as far as he knows."

The American added, "Which means there has to be a glitch somewhere in the Iranian apparatus. That's you. He'll come after you."

"Is that why the gun?"

"That's one of the reasons. Also, America is a dangerous playground. Lots of cowboys. Once you feel the noose tighten, call us," the American said as they started to leave the room.

Sami shouted at the American, "Who do I ask for, Mr. . . . ?"

"Caspar the Friendly Fucking Ghost."

The bright lamp, the interrogating tape recorder, the handcuffs—all gone in a flash. He sat at the table for a half hour with his eyes closed.

He could still feel the chill that had run through him when Musavi had called the rest of them out of the van to come inside. The Libyan had then held Sami back to let Abdul-Karim, Hazrat, and Zuheir go in first. He figured the other Libyans must have been working with Musavi and the American all along without really knowing what the agenda was. That probably made it three point-blank shots at Abdul-Karim, Hazrat, and Zuheir. Three kills that would save the unwitting United States Department of Justice a whole lot of headaches, while raising the interesting possibility that the American in the gray suit might be some sort of deep-cover counterintelligence type acting the part of a renegade businessman. Not an implausible theory, but Sami did not believe it for a second. This was a lot simpler than that. One of the Arab *Mukhabarat*, for instance, might have its own shadow tailing it, as the Office did to the Iranian security service. But if that was really the case and Musavi was working for an Arab counterpart of the Office, then who the devil was the American? With the Israelis, maybe? No, because Musavi was too much of an Arab and, besides, the Israelis had nothing to gain by protecting the American taxpayer against the Moslem brotherhood on this side of the Atlantic. If anything, the reverse was true.

Sami sighed. The H&K's magazine had ten rounds in it. Spec-op military-type pistol modified for civilian use. Top of the line. He could sell a pistol like this for a small fortune back in Tehran. Which meant, 1) the American was way too generous; 2) he really wanted Sami to survive; 3) he wanted Sami to be saddled with a murder weapon; 4) none of the above.

Sami pulled himself up with difficulty. It was a big empty concrete space he found himself in. A few odd pieces of furniture here and there and nothing more. He looked at his watch: already past seven o'clock and no point in hurrying to Times Square for the Colonel's next phone call. He pushed on the heavy door and stepped out into the night air. There was a lot of commotion on the other side of the street around the building where the window display was. He saw people going in and out, some standing by the steps smoking cigarettes. The door was open and inside the building was very brightly lit. It was the only building on the entire block that was lit at all and Sami, knowing full well that approaching it was a bad idea, was attracted to it like a moth to candlelight.

He felt invisible. Nobody even bothered to give him a second look inside that crowded place, even though he knew his beat-up face must look like hamburger meat by now. The first thing he noticed was a long table topped with edibles: cheese, crackers, small pastries, potato chips, coffee, and red and white wine. There were a series of medium-sized photographs on the nearest wall. The exact same pictures—he realized after a closer look—of a small white terrier in a single pose, though juxtaposed with different colored backgrounds. In the middle of the space someone had thrown a good five dozen pieces of brick in haphazard fashion. Bricks. Just bricks, he thought, nonplussed. Then he wormed his way through the crowd to where someone had laid out a number of plaster penises with crosses filed into stakes driven through them. He'd never seen anything like it. It was enough to put a school of *tullabs*, Moslem student preachers, over the edge for good.

"What do you think?"

A tiny woman, maybe forty or so, with dark frizzy hair and intense brown eyes was standing next to him.

Not being quite sure what she meant, he asked, "What is this place?"

"This place?"

"Yes, I mean what is all this?"

"This is an art gallery, an opening for a group show. A group show," she emphasized a second time. "The work over there, the photographs, that's mine."

"The dogs?"

"*A* dog. One dog. Franny. Franny's mouth."

Now Sami wasn't sure if he should commit himself to laughter or serious talk, mainly because he didn't know whether the woman was putting him on. His jawbone hurt too much to laugh anyway. A group of three people strolled by and congratulated the woman on her "piece." They called her Paula. Paula was a slightly attractive woman wearing too much lipstick. Her nail polish, he noticed, was the color of her flat blue shoes.

"What do you think?" she asked a second time.

"What I think . . . I thought people didn't ask these kinds of questions so bluntly."

"Well, I'm asking."

"Very good. Your pictures are very good."

"Then you'll let me take yours?"

"Why would you want to take my picture?"

"Because you look like a truck just ran over you."

Suddenly he was pissed off at himself for having walked into this place, standing out like a sore thumb among people who would be able to describe him for weeks to come. And to top it off, this woman wanted to take his picture.

"Maybe they have a bathroom I could use to clean up," he said.

"No, no. I want you just like this. What's your name?"

"Peter."

"Peter, I'm Paula. Listen to me, I'll take you home right now and take a roll of film just as you are. I can't pay you, but you'll get a signed copy of yourself when my next show comes out."

"What will you call it? *Peter's Bruises*?"

"If you like."

"I just want to wash my face a bit. The bruises won't go away with a little cold water, you know."

He'd barely known this strange woman for five minutes and it already felt as if he was obligated to explain himself to her. He left her by the plaster penises and asked around until someone showed him the bathroom. He locked himself inside and took a few deep breaths, trying to get his bearings for a minute. In the mirror he saw that he didn't look half as bad as he thought he should, though obviously bad enough to qualify as a subject for Paula out there. His pockets were empty. His passport was still intact in the hidden pocket beneath his pants, but the money in his front pocket was gone. He realized the big Arab must have taken it from him while he was out. He muttered, "Son of a bitch," unsure if he was directing the curse at the Arab for taking his last three hundred dollars or the Colonel for leaving him out in the cold like this. Then again, maybe he was directing it at Musavi and the American for confusing him, or the supposedly dead Abdul-Karim and his Sunday terrorists for stirring up all this nonsense in the first place.

The bottom line right now was money. He felt faint with hunger and thirst. He could go prowl around for old Joanna at the AfterBurner bar or he could take up this other woman's offer and see where it would lead him for the night. When he came out of the bathroom, Paula was standing guard right outside, as if afraid he might escape her clutches somehow.

"What do you say?"

"I say I look like a boxer who took a few shots but still came out on top."

Her face brightened up all of a sudden. "That's it. That's what we'll call your portrait: *The Boxer Who Took a Few Shots but Still Came Out on Top.*"

He ended up falling asleep in a sitting position on her couch. The whole time he was dimly aware of movement around the small living room and of bright light shining on his closed eyelids. He had a dream he was back in that warehouse being interviewed by a tape recorder in a multitude of languages. He dreamt about Paula's group show and more bright lights.

When he woke up Billie Holiday was singing on the radio and the lighting was dimmed. He looked around and saw that she had boxed him in a corner surrounded with reflector cloth. The clock on the wall showed four—four in the morning, he assumed. It was a cuckoo clock but with the cuckoo left out of its box and bent to the side. Paula wasn't in the living room.

While Billie sang he tiptoed over the books scattered on the floor to the fridge and took out whatever he could find inside. One egg, bacon slices, some hardened baguette, and a bowl of cottage cheese. He ate indiscriminately, swallowing the raw egg whole, then lapping up the cheese with some bread, and finally chewing on the uncooked bacon right out of the wrapper. He hadn't had bacon since the missionary school. The moist, slightly slippery, thin and uncooked meat in his mouth felt something akin to a sexual act.

The thought reminded him again of his friend Mozart from the Western Europe Desk. One of Mozart's words of advice about going on assignment in America had been to "make sure to sleep with an American woman. There is something cosmic in that, my friend, let me tell you. It's not like you are making love with just one woman, but as if you were making love to all of America. It's a different a feeling. It's vast, brother. It's like Christopher Columbus."

He missed Mozart. Why? Why now? Probably because Mozart could always find his niche in whatever environment he found himself in. Even his operational name, *Mozart*, was a brilliant device, wasn't it? In a fantastic way it granted him leeway with superiors, as if he really *were* some composing genius who must be cut more slack than others.

Sami thought, And what does a man like Mozart, or even the Colonel, have to do with me? Nothing, of course. He understood that his one facility lay in knowing how to grab on to the coattails of better jugglers than himself. Otherwise, what really was there for him in Tehran? Not a whole a lot. His so-called foreign features made him suspect to most people in the Middle East. And yet here in New York where he could easily blend in, he felt like a creature from another planet. How could he even begin to describe to anyone the trajectory of a life that had brought him from the Iranian Army draft board to a highly secret intelligence department of that same country, and now to folks who stuck crosses into plaster penises in New York City and actually made their living taking pictures of poodles and beat-up faces?

"You eat like a barbarian," Paula told him. She was standing outside the bathroom door with a yellow towel wrapped around her waist and a man's silk shirt on.

"Christopher Columbus."

"What did you say?"

"I'm no Christopher Columbus."

"Speaking in riddles, huh? I took a whole roll of film of you sitting on that couch. What is it you do for a living?"

"I'm a systems analyst. I read tarot cards. I coach in the soccer league."

Paula walked up to him. She looked like a spinster who hadn't aged at all badly. In fact she was quite an improvement over Joanna at the bar. Now he realized why Mozart had said that thing about making love to America. It really was the thing to say, wasn't it? Every day men in cities like Tehran dreamt of the fair flesh of American and European females, as if they could be graced through that intercourse and become a little less unappetizing themselves. And they came back from whatever murderous assignments they were given to complete with tales that had to do with their conquering lower parts. Oh, if Paula here had any idea just how to the point those plaster penises at the gallery opening had really been! Those penises with stakes shaped like crosses driven through them. If he ever made it back to Tehran, he'd tell Mozart about this: I didn't get to make love to America, but I did see mangled pricks. And I understood. It took a while, but I understood.

"You know why I brought you to my house tonight? Because you looked like an orphan. You looked lost. Who beat you up tonight?"

"Some kids. They took my money. That sort of thing."

His answer seemed to disappoint Paula, as if she'd expected something much more dramatic than that. She lost interest quickly. By next week all she would remember of him would be his pummeled face on a roll of Kodak film.

Now without warning she came up to him and grabbed his crotch. The move was so sudden that he winced and automatically made to push her away.

She looked offended. "Hey, take it easy. You're not some escaped weirdo, are you? You're not going to hurt me, I hope."

Her words had no force behind them, as if they were little weightless balloons that one sent up into the air to see float and disappear.

He felt a sudden singular revulsion for this woman. It came from nowhere and masked his face.

"What is it?"

"Nothing. I'm sorry."

Now he sensed that he had lent her disappointment in him enough self-sufficiency so that she could go to bed without fearing he would violate her in any way. And she did just that, retreated from him without saying another word. The trouble was, he was starting to nurture his own clumsiness. Why had he come here in the first place? Going with the flow and playing it their way as the Colonel had said was one thing, but cultivating a damned identity crisis in the middle of an operation was stupid, not to mention unforgivable.

Half an hour passed. Paula was asleep in her bedroom. Sami opened and closed the fridge a couple of times. He leafed through some art books while listening to old jazz on the radio.

I could live here, he thought—in America.

He found three different cameras in the living room alone. It couldn't be helped, he had to peek in the bedroom, too, to be sure. The door to her room was ajar and a low wall lamp was on. An invitation maybe? Or a false sense of security? He took a quick glance from where he was standing. No more cameras. Back in the living room he emptied the rolls from each camera and put them in his pocket. Sorry! But that's how it had to be. There was about a dollar and a half's worth of change on one of the stereo speakers. He took that, too, and put it in his pocket. Enough for two cups of coffee until eight o'clock tonight when his next call should come.

Outside it would be cold.

7

NEW YORK IS COLD, but I like where I'm living. Huh! I guess if you got nowhere to go, then that means New York is just cold."

It was nearing eight o'clock in the evening. Sami's feet had gone to sleep nearly an hour earlier. Cold hardly did justice to how it felt outside. Once, during an unlikely fit of physical courage, he'd made a run to Damadi's place to see if he could find the man, but Damadi had disappeared altogether. Desperate, he'd even considered going back to the safe house of Musavi's Libyans in Brooklyn to get some sleep. Better yet, he might contact Section Nineteen in Tehran and give them some cockeyed story about getting ambushed so as to have an excuse to return to Tehran. But he knew that Zaheri and his people from Nineteen would not buy this for a second, and probably were on to the fact that Sami was a mole from the Office.

Otherwise why would Damadi, his supposed contact from Nineteen, have disappeared all of a sudden without telling him anything?

"Hey, you're not listening to me. What's my name?"

Sami looked at the old guy who had been lecturing him about horse racing for the past two hours, a fast-talking dawdler with a fisherman's cap and a huge appetite for coffee and sugar.

"You're Goldberg," he answered absentmindedly.

"No. Goldie, son. Goldie. What was I telling you?"

Sami looked at his watch again, an act that Goldie picked up too quickly, as if his life's meaning lay in keeping people from looking at their watches.

"You were telling me about how New York is cold but you like where you're living."

"No. That was a manner of speech. I was telling you about how the triple-double works. That's a betting term."

"Tell me some other time."

Sami downed the remains of a flavorless coffee that had grown cold. He'd sat in this side-street delicatessen on 43rd Street for most of the day, killing time and listening in on preposterous conversations of stooping, vitamin-starved men and women who looked like they'd just been released from a bankrupt freak and variety show. Broadway/Times Square was just a couple of restaurants away and the *New York Times* Building happened to be across the street, yet for all that stood around it, this place could have existed in another dimension.

The delicatessen was a twenty-four-hour joint mainly frequented by luckless old whores, down-and-out offtrack-betting losers, and transvestites who hung out in front of the seedy Carter Hotel up near Eighth Avenue. Once in a while one of the blue-collar printers from the *New York Times* Building would venture in for a doughnut and a cup of coffee and throw a poisonous glance around. The Indian countermen seemed to get a special kick out of their regulars, since they didn't bother to boot out anybody who lingered too long. It was a marvel how much you could pick up from the life of a single Manhattan block within a few hours, as if the even division of the streets created perfectly self-contained cycles and rhythms from one block to the next, so much so that Sami already felt like he'd been an inhabitant of this particular turf forever.

He left Goldie at his table and braced himself for the wait outside. The telephone behind the police station kiosk did not ring until 8:04.

"Yahya," the Colonel said.

"I want to come back in. My job is finished. Not that I had anything to do with it. You should know that better than anyone else."

"What's that supposed to mean?"

"They're collecting maggots, all those geniuses I came here to watch."

"How did they get it?"

"They got it from your Lemon friend. Who is he and why wasn't I told we had extra men on board? Or am I even asking the right questions?"

"You are. Except there was no need for you to know until you had to know. That's how the game is played. Besides, *they* came to *me*. It was a last-minute thing and we all figured we shared the same interest."

"Fair enough. Now tell me, when do I get back?"

"You don't."

"What?"

"You hang up the phone. You walk due west. You buy the day's *New York Post* on your way. You walk three blocks. You come to an intersection. You turn right. Immediately as you turn you look for a postbox with a chalk mark. The rest you know. Walk up to the next block and stand in front of a telephone booth near a well-lit parking lot. The phone will ring in . . . fifteen minutes. When you've finished on the telephone you walk over and stand by the parking lot and you hold the newspaper upside down. Good-bye."

That was it?

His bafflement turned to slight panic when he found out that the newsstand on the other side of Broadway was out of the *Post*. But then Goldie came to mind. Every one of those racing junkies sitting in the delicatessen on 43rd Street carried a copy of the *Post* in their pockets. He ran back inside.

"Hey, Goldie!"

"Who are you?"

The paper was rolled up in Goldie's side pocket.

"Goldie, let me see the race results again."

"Buy your own, asshole."

"I will. But not today."

After he had wrestled the paper out of Goldie's hands and was on his way out, he realized he didn't have the fifty cents to buy his own paper. He hurried past Eighth and Ninth Avenues. On Tenth he looked and saw the chalk mark on the mailbox. Two minutes later the phone rang on the corner of 44th and Tenth.

He didn't bother with formalities. "Who is Musavi? Who is the American?"

"Musavi is a Libyan operative gone private," the Colonel answered. "The American's name—well, his name doesn't matter."

"It does to me."

"We know him as Joe Havelock. No doubt he has intelligence background. But it's hard to tell. An arms dealer to the Libyans. But not exclusively. Sudan, too, maybe a few other places."

"Are we secure on this thing?"

"As secure as we're ever going to get. Which is not saying much."

"You're telling me there is an American crazy enough to go into business with the Libyans after what happened ten years ago?"

"Listen, that's none of our business. Anyway, I suppose his theory is: what better business to go into than one nobody else dares to touch."

Sami puzzled the rest of it silently to himself while the Colonel gave him time to do so. Okay, so the Arab Musavi and the American Havelock were on our side. Why? Because Havelock didn't want his lucrative dealings interrupted in any way. And they *would* be if the U.S. Customs and Treasury Departments started delving too deeply into Middle Eastern affairs. In the meantime, through Musavi, Havelock had found out there just happened to be a bunch of Arabs out to cause mayhem in America. So he had teamed up with the Office—with the Colonel—to rear-end the infamous Mosque Connection.

No way. This line of reasoning was not strong enough; it had no punch. Yet he was in no mood to continue to sort through more equations. He asked, "When can I come back?"

"You don't. You stay put. You hold your newspaper upside down and you wait."

"No!"

The Colonel continued as if Sami hadn't spoken. "You'll receive your orders shortly."

He stood in front of the parking lot. It was too difficult trying to read anything upside down, so he gave it up after a while. Everybody looked suspect. He checked out a couple of Hispanic men drinking beer on the steps to his right. There was the parking lot attendant himself, a thin Chinese fellow who appeared to be getting ready to come nosing around. An elderly man passed by next. Then a long-haired blond couple carrying backpacks and passing a joint back and forth. By nine o'clock he was sure he must be the coldest Iranian operative who ever tried to read an upside-down newspaper on Tenth Avenue. A young black kid asked him if he had a cigarette to spare. The answer was no, though that was one habit he could have really used right now.

When she finally bumped into him he went down with the back of his skull aiming for the pavement. She cushioned it with her hand easily.

Immediately, straddling him deftly from above, dressed in a pair of tight leather pants, she said, "I'm sorry, but Yahya is who?"

"Yahya is John the fucking Baptist. Now, could you please get off me?"

They stood there for a full minute, eyeballing each other.

"You're dry-cleaned," she said, "so go ahead and stare as long as you want. I have to admit, though, you don't know how to wait very well."

He was speechless. This leather-clad American woman with the spiked blond hair and liquid brown eyes that refused to give into his stare was supposed to be his contact in New York City? He knew she knew what he was thinking, so he didn't even try to be discreet about the extent of his shock. An oversized American car halted on the other side of the street. For a minute he thought it was all a big mix-up. Any second now a couple of federal agents would jump out of that car to read him his rights before he was handcuffed. Within the hour FBI C-I officers would be arguing with headquarters in D.C. about whether they could try and turn the Iranian.

Nothing of the sort. A middle-aged couple got out of the car and went about their business.

"I have a busy night ahead," she said. "Are you coming or what?"

She hailed a cab down and gave the driver an address on 53rd and First.

During the ride he checked her out. She was used to that, you could tell. Had she been to Iran? Was that where the Colonel had picked her up. It seemed unlikely. He found himself gawking at the smoothness of her curves too hungrily, unable to shake off the leverage she already seemed to have gained on him.

Her apartment was on the second floor of a renovated walkup on 53rd Street. It was a bigger place than he'd expected. There were two bedrooms and a large kitchen. The living room was fairly bare: a small boom box on the floor, a tall bookcase, and some stuffed pillows thrown into corners on the hardwood floor. She disappeared into her bedroom and came back with some clothes for him.

"How do you know my size?"

"Just wear them, okay? The shower works, use it. There's no shaving cream, but you can use soap. Food's in the fridge.

Here's twenty dollars. Order some pizza if you like. But no salami on it. It's not kosher—I mean, it's not *halal.* Wait a minute, are you a devout Moslem?"

"I'm not a devout anything."

"Didn't think so. Order what you like, then." She started to walk away, then changed her mind and turned around. "What's your name?"

"You already know that. But okay, Sami."

"Ellena. I was told you'd be an Iranian."

"I am."

"You don't look it."

"My mother . . . was an American."

"Sami!" she teased too quickly, "I'm disappointed in you. You shouldn't divulge secrets so casually. That's a very American thing to do. Don't you know that?"

"You asked, I answered. I couldn't care less if I was begotten by Martians."

"Your English is excellent."

"Is that a question?"

"Yes."

"I was raised in a missionary school in Tehran. I've also watched a shitload of gangster movies, for research purposes, of course."

"Sami, you really have to stop giving away your secrets like that."

"Are you through playing games?"

"That hurt! Here's an extra set of keys. I'll be back late." She pointed to his room. "It's yours. Make yourself comfortable." She started to leave again, carrying a big gym bag under her arm.

"Maybe we ought to discuss a few things. I mean, I haven't come here to have a picnic, you know."

"Relax, Mr. Amir. I have a job to go to. A regular job, not a cover. And it so happens that this regular job starts at night. Eat your nonkosher pizza and we'll talk in the morning."

Then she was gone.

He ended up getting the pizza himself from an Original Ray's on First Avenue. Afterwards he shaved and took a long bath. He wouldn't have minded if she never returned. He could see himself occupying this spacious apartment for a long time to come—taking quick jaunts down to the pizza shop, watching American television in peace and quiet, making coffee with freshly ground beans, getting himself a job that was mindless yet regular. All the things that were taken for granted in this other hemisphere.

He wondered whether the Office was *making use* of his own apartment in Tehran right now. It was one of those solidly built prerevolution structures above Vali-asr Square where he could play the jazz CDs he'd brought back from Europe as loud as he wanted to. In the afternoons the neighborhood high school girls would giggle nervously as he passed by and the kids playing soccer on the block would point him out to each other and call out in French, "Monsieur," convinced that he was a foreigner.

He fell asleep watching a nature film about elephants. In the morning when he woke up, the door to his room was shut but the small television was still on, showing a fat Santa Claus posing in front of the Rockefeller Center Christmas tree. It was already past eleven. He wandered around the apartment in his new clothes. Ellena wasn't in and her bedroom door was wide open. Outside, it was sunny but appeared very cold. He turned the stove on for some hot water. The kitchen, he thought, appeared too neat, not much used at all. A brown teddy bear was sitting on top of the kitchen table. He found himself thinking, What kind of a person would have a teddy bear in her kitchen?

Once the water had boiled, he turned it off without bothering to look for coffee. Then he was in her bedroom, drawn to it because it was there. If he ever made it back to the Office, he could tell Mozart about his progress with the women of this great big country: first there was homely Joanna in whose apartment he had spent the night, then semifair Paula who had wanted to take his photograph, and finally lovely Ellena who was as of yet a riddle.

She had a writing desk in her bedroom with paper strewn all over it. It took him a while to realize that they were unsuccessful poems she'd torn out of her notebook but never gotten around to throwing away. Loath to part with them, perhaps? He opened one of the drawers to the desk, his eye immediately caught by a Polaroid photograph lying over a heap of diary type notebooks. It was a picture of a swarthy young man with a serious face posing in front of the Eiffel Tower. Arab, he thought.

A knock came on the bedroom door.

"You won't find any souvenirs in my bedroom."

"I'm sorry. I was just . . ."

"*Poking around* is the word. Did you find anything interesting?"

Sami shook his head. Her sarcasm was searching to take root, as if she begrudged the welcome she had to extend to him.

"I'm sorry," he said again.

In the kitchen she repeated her question. "Did you find anything interesting in my room?"

"I don't make a habit of it."

"That wasn't my question."

"Listen, obviously you're an American. I don't know how or why you came to be associated with us, but I'm sure nobody forced you into it. And nobody is forcing you now. If you're unhappy about it, I'll leave."

"How do you know no one is forcing me?"

"I don't. I'm guessing."

"What do you take with it?"

She'd put a cup of steaming coffee in front of him. He was thinking this was the first noninvasive thing she had said to him since they'd met. But then she added, "You're not very good at this, are you?"

"Were you my contact all along, then? Are you the one who didn't show up by the statue?"

"You had a tail. I watched you."

"It was Musavi and Havelock, or whatever their names are. How much do you know about all this anyway?"

"Ask me," she said.

Her clothes were a far cry from what she'd had on last night. With that plain white blouse and those gray slacks, she could be dressed for some type of an office job right now. He couldn't be sure whether she had been assigned to make him uncomfortable on purpose or whether she just enjoyed it.

"Does the name Firuz ring a bell?" he asked carefully.

She caught on right away. "No, but Zaheri does. Listen, you don't need to test me to know if my need-to-know is up and current. Just ask and you'll receive."

Sami sipped his coffee. It tasted good, so much better than what he'd had yesterday sitting with Goldie at that delicatessen on 43rd Street.

"It sounds stupid, but thank you for everything. I was pretty desperate yesterday."

"Don't mention it. It all goes on the expense account." She laughed. "Eggs and toast?"

He nodded. There was silence for some time while she cooked for the two of them. Once they were both sitting down again, he said, "Okay then, tell me about Zaheri."

"Section Nineteen. Don't look so surprised. This American will never give your secrets away, Mr. Amir."

"Never say never."

"I can relate to that, of course. But did you ever ask yourself how Nineteen would entrust you with an American assignment after only being with them for half a year?"

He couldn't help it, he was surprised again. She knew too many things that were not necessary for her to know. Usually this would mean she was either screwing someone over at the Europe desk or she was screwing the Colonel himself. But he doubted both.

"How is it you know the Office had me planted at Nineteen only six months ago?"

"There you go again. I know it's difficult, but you have to get used to it: *I'm* your contact here. If I were a man and an Iranian, you wouldn't be trying so hard to figure me out, would you?"

"It's a little irregular."

"It's *very* irregular, from what I understand. But you'll have to get used to it."

"I have."

"Good. Zaheri and Nineteen knew all along you were a plant from the Office. They know you guys have been watching them for years. You *have* been, haven't you?"

Sami said nothing to that.

She lit a cigarette. "I can see I'm going to have to earn your trust, Mr. Amir."

"Sami will do. And I'm sorry, it's habit. I know what you're trying to tell me. Zaheri and people like him want to keep American pressure on Iran. That's one way for them to stay in power. They're nervous as hell with the elections coming up. And they'd like nothing better than for a Nimitz-class to send a couple of F-15s over Iranian air. Anything for them to have an excuse to get mad and get their Basij morons out onto the streets. There's nothing new about all this. It's an open secret all the way from Tehran to the D.C. suburbs."

"You talk like an article from *Foreign Affairs*."

"I've had to translate plenty of their articles."

"Impressive. Maybe we could get you a job on C-SPAN."

"Maybe."

"How would you like to go for a walk?"

"Love to."

Twenty minutes later they were standing above the FDR Drive and the East River, talking again. Ellena asked him what he was laughing about.

"It's strange, in New York you walk a couple of blocks and it's as if you'd traveled to another city altogether. Look at how peaceful it is around here. It almost makes you want to write poetry."

She turned to him. "Those papers in my room, they weren't really poems. Just silly stuff."

"Hey, you don't have to apologize to me. I was translating poetry for a living before I got into this business."

"And are you happy you made the switch?"

He shrugged. "Most the poets I met were assholes anyway. No offense."

She asked, "Do you have a gun?"

"You know I do. Last night your hands were all over it when you bumped into me."

"You'll have to use it. Zaheri is on his way to New York."

"You can't be serious?"

The very prospect of having to do the Office's messy work out here in New York made him queasy.

"They never told me I was getting hired to pull this kind of shit," he muttered.

She smiled at his contrived naïveté. "Did you expect them to?"

He shrugged.

She went on. "Like I told you, Zaheri and Nineteen had known all along about you. You were the fall guy for New York, set up to get caught working with the Arabs. Do you realize what the remotest possibility of another bombing like the World Trade Center would do to public opinion here?"

"I have an idea."

"Then afterwards Zaheri was going to turn around and use the news of your capture to prey on the Office back in Tehran—blow the whole network wide open, so to speak."

"This is all guesswork."

"It's what I've been told. I haven't been told *why* it's so important for Zaheri to come all the way out here. But they say he's coming. And you've got your orders. You'll get a call at eight tonight for details."

"And you?"

"What about me?"

"Why are you so abstract about who has spoken to you? Your only real connection is the Colonel, isn't it?"

"Why do you say that?" she asked, turning away from him.

"Because it's his style to put people like you and me on the payroll."

"You mean we're birds of a feather?"

"I don't know this expression."

"Yes, you do. It means we're twins, philosophically speaking, of course."

"Of course. Birds of a feather."

There was so much he was still uncertain about. After he'd had the afternoon to sort through it all, he realized the balance was still in favor of all the things that hadn't been disclosed yet. Three things bothered him most:

First, why should Havelock and Musavi trouble themselves with outright murder just because they didn't want anyone to snoop into things Libyan? This didn't add up at all. Even now there were American companies making on-the-books fortunes off Gadhafi's enormous tunnel project in the Saharan desert without being harassed by the American government.

Second, as the Section Nineteen head, Zaheri was taking an extreme measure by coming to New York: it was the type of move a section head would make only when stakes were very high—if even then. And despite everything that had happened until now, Sami had never thought of this trip, from the Office's point of view, as anything but routine: *Make sure we are not left with Moslem terrorist photos on the cover of the* New York Times.

Which brought him to the third and most sensitive part of the puzzle so far: where did Nur fit in all of this? And if he fit anywhere at all, why hadn't Ellena brought his name up? Sami had bluffed silence on that topic to see Ellena's reaction. If she had taken the initiative to mention Nur's name, it would have meant that the Office was genuinely concerned with more than just assassinating the head of Section Nineteen, Zaheri, once he got to New York. But since she hadn't said a word about Nur, the contrary explanation became doubly probable. Maybe the Colonel's agenda had less to do with stopping a bomber like Nur than eliminating a rival like Zaheri.

In any case, it was starting to look as if Sami's real assignment for the time being was simply to wait. So much of the last few years he'd spent waiting. It was in the nature of the work. And yet waiting never got any easier, did it?

She had given him another four hundred dollars. He stuck that inside his right shoe. Then he took a look around, his attention wandering automatically to her private quarters. Her bedroom door was shut; apparently she was asleep, or maybe she was busy tearing unsuccessful poems out of her notebook. Her calm was like a capsized boat over which he couldn't balance himself. Had Mozart or any of the guys from the Office been here, they would have already been knocking on her door. "Let me in!" And he could just see her turning from her writing desk long enough to answer, "I knew you couldn't keep your hands off your dick for too long, silly little man from the East!"

It was drizzling outside, yet for lack of anything better to do he decided to step back out on the street. He walked slowly west past the Museum of Modern Art. For years he'd heard about this famous place, but now that he was right by its doors he had no appetite to go inside. Mozart had told him about moments like this: the job's existential downtime, when an agent afloat couldn't be sure if he was betting against the house itself or anyone in particular. But Father O'Malley, too, had told him something. Back at the missionary school the old man had often spoken of *divine spaces*, spaces where a troubled soul could cull his drifting selves, amass himself at the root. So by the time Sami had made a loop in his walk and come face-to-face with the great edifice of Saint Patrick's Cathedral on 50th Street and Fifth Avenue, he knew exactly what he had to do.

The avenue swarmed with Christmas shoppers while people poured in and out of the cathedral's portals. This impulse to enter was not as sudden as he would have liked to believe. After all, visiting the Lord's house was waiting made easier, was it not?

Inside, his reflexes from missionary-school days took over. He dipped his finger in the holy water and made the sign of the cross.

Take this, all of you, and eat it: this is my body which will be given up for you.

Drilled memories.

Take this, all of you, and drink from it: this is the cup of my blood, the blood of the new and everlasting covenant. It will be shed for you and for all so that sins may be forgiven. Do this in memory of me.

He dropped a dollar in the offertory box and lit a votive candle.

Remember, Lord, those who have died and have gone before us marked with the sign of faith, especially those for whom we now pray. . . .

Here, Father O'Malley's name came to his tongue.

It really was true: waiting played terrible havoc with one's mind. He stared at his watch. It was barely past noon now and he had another eight very slow hours to go before taking the Colonel's next call.

"So?"

Sami was determined not to be intimidated with all the guesswork being thrown in his direction. The Colonel must have decided for a particular reason to wait a full twenty-four hours before giving him the details of what had to be done with Zaheri. And that reason could not be the fear of an NSA/GCHQ wiretap, not if he was going to reveal to Sami tonight what he could have told him yesterday. No, the real reason had to be that the boss wanted him to be thrown off guard for one night. To have his Ellena experience, so to speak. Why? He didn't know. But he found it distasteful enough to completely avoid mentioning her now. And the Colonel, on his part, reciprocated, since he no doubt hated the gift of voluntary explanations.

Sami started by asking about Zaheri.

"Why would the man come all the way out here himself?"

He realized that the Colonel must be torn between loyalty to the idea that a superior officer should not be asked these sorts of questions and the fact that he needed Sami to complete a task on which the Office's very survival probably depended.

"He's coming because he's a worried man."

"Aren't we all."

The Colonel sighed into the telephone. "Zaheri and Havelock are competitors. There's a lot of bad blood."

"You mean to tell me Nineteen has been dealing in the trade?" This was understood to be the arms trade.

"Not the whole organization. Just Zaheri. He's been stealing overstock from the Sepah and shipping it here and there, mostly through Lebanon."

Sami stared for a few seconds at the cheap encryption device over the receiver. Then he asked, "Are you sure we're safe?"

"I told you that before."

He knew the Colonel really meant that it didn't matter one way or another. It was the paradox of signals intelligence that when the cards were all stacked in favor of your opponent, it was more advantageous sometimes to be overheard than not overheard. The Colonel couldn't have cared less if Zaheri's name came up a dozen times in their conversation. In fact, he would have welcomed it. As for Havelock, that had to be a phony name anyway.

So the scenario had changed: Zaheri was coming over here not because his little American operation was botched, but because of *who* had botched it for him, namely Havelock, the American arms runner and businessman. He wanted to be finished, once and for all, with this particular thorn in his side.

Sami asked, "But how would Zaheri know that Havelock had anything to do with what happened here?"

"Don't be stupid. We leaked it to him on purpose. How do you think it's done?"

"And he's dumb enough to fall for this?"

"Desperate people do desperate things sometimes."

"How do I find him?"

"Use your imagination."

Sami thought he'd found an angle. "But why rough me up if they're with us—Havelock and Musavi, I mean?"

"I wouldn't know. Ask them when you see them."

The inevitable click came. He wondered whether the Colonel's last words meant he should call Havelock for assistance—826-6585—or bide his time. He'd call, he decided, but only if he must.

8

OPENED TO ITS MIDDLE, the good-sized English-Arabic dictionary he'd picked at random from her bookshelf rested on his chest like a pet made out of parchment. He remained motionless on the living room floor. It was three in the morning and snowing lightly outside. He'd turned the light off hours ago but still held on to the book as if a vocabular miracle might take place, allowing him to ingest an entire language while he dozed.

The outside lock turned. He didn't stir. He saw her silhouette hesitate before his door. Then she put a foot inside and quickly retreated, as if unwilling to give up the advantage of surprise. He followed her with his eyes as she went inside her bedroom. A few minutes passed. He could hear the sound of running water in the shower. Then she reappeared again, naked from the waist up. She went into the kitchen to get something out of the fridge. From his vantage point he could plainly see the sweep of her breasts as she brought her neck back a little to drink from the bottle she had picked out, one hand resting on her left hip in an almost defiant attitude, as if she were challenging the very thought of prying eyes.

As he watched her he recalled the picture of the handsome young Arab he'd seen in her desk drawer. A familiar face, he thought: typical young Arab male aching to make his mark through the haze of a lifetime of real and imaginary grievances. You could usually find him in any one of a dozen European capitals where he'd been sent by his family to study engineering or medicine, yet somewhere along the line fate would deal him an unkind slap and before long he'd be turned into a PFLP sleeper or a low-ranking member of the murderous gang of Abu Nidal.

Sami wondered if the Arab in that picture had been around long enough to see her like this, her fine white body in a graceful odd-hour pose, and the young man thanking the lucky stars that had brought the glamorous life to the heart of his Jordanian village past, so that he could possess a Christian woman and play terrorist at the same time, convinced that the crusade he fought was of a subtler kind.

"Do you like what you see?"

She had stopped on her way back to the bedroom, turned around, and spoken to him as if she were picking up from the middle of a conversation left off.

"The question makes me uncomfortable," he said honestly.

"Oh? Then tell me, how did you ever get involved in this business?"

"I saw an ad in the newspaper. Your water's getting cold."

After he had heard her closing the bathroom door he got up and entered her bedroom. The torn pages of poetry were still there, some of them shredded beyond comprehension, but there were a few bits and pieces that were nearly whole.

He read,

Her days bent
an instrument.

and she knows about fading
and the lover listening
how simple she would like to be
whispering:
I am simple. I am simple.

He thought, *Bent* and *instrument* rhyme. So do *fading* and *listening*. Other than that, what? At one time he'd been paid to translate poetry but never to analyze their lines.

The next quarter of a page had been made illegible, then she'd written:

To the king she says
I will poison you one day
and the king says
I am your slave, I am your slave

When he heard her coming out of the shower, he didn't bother to leave, letting his eyes stay focused on the scratches of paper in his hand.

This time she wouldn't break the silence.

Without looking up, he commented, "The repetitions in your poem of 'I am your slave' and 'I am simple' mirror one another, I guess."

"And who's 'the king'?"

"I heard, or maybe I read it somewhere—I'm not sure—that A'isha, the Prophet's wife, said the same thing to the Prophet once. What do you think?"

"A'isha! Who's A'isha?"

"I told you, the Prophet's wife. Then again, maybe you're A'isha."

"What do you want?"

He finally looked up at her. She had on a white bathrobe and she appeared to shine. It was a recurring punctuation mark, this alien feeling he had; this was her house, her country, her failed poetry, and ultimately he was *her* charge. Now he imagined her standing next to the Colonel lighting the man's pipe. He felt like saying to her, You're blue like ice, not quite knowing what that meant.

"I didn't ask the Colonel about you, if you'd like to know."

"Why not?"

"I didn't want to give him the pleasure of being asked."

She laughed. "Do you compete with him?"

"No, of course not. But you were dumped on me. I'm not saying this to be unpleasant. But you wouldn't know what I'm talking about unless you came from where I come from."

"You're half American, though."

"That means nothing. I was raised over there. I learned how to be thoroughly fucked up over there."

"Okay, fair enough. Do you want to hear my story now?"

"I'm content to know it's there for me to hear when I want it."

"Then do you mind if I put my clothes on?"

"I've already seen what there is to see."

She shrugged. "Suit yourself."

She slipped on the black tank top lying on her bed and took out a pair of mustard-colored jogging pants from a drawer.

"How about something to eat?"

He nodded okay to that.

Half an hour later when they met again in the kitchen with the steaming all-night Chinese delivery food between them, she asked, "How are you going to find Zaheri?"

"I'll have to let him come to me. I'm going to perch at Damadi's place for a while."

"Who's that?"

He thought she did a fine job of making it sound like a genuine question.

"Nineteen's man in New York. How is it your so-called need-to-know doesn't reach to a rodent like Damadi?"

"Maybe I wasn't fucking the Colonel hard enough on the night he was to have told me about it."

He stayed silent. Despite himself he felt a choke in his throat. Ellena caught it.

"I was just kidding. I don't fuck people for information. It's not as if my life depended on this job, and even if it did, I'd think hard before I went that far. Would *you* go that far?"

"I always thought this job *was* fucking people for information."

She had to smile at that. "Tell me about the Middle East."

"The Middle East is a big place."

"Then tell me about Iran."

He had to wait to finish chewing on his rubbery piece of

fried broccoli. Then he answered, " 'Things fall apart; the centre cannot hold.' It's that sort of a place."

"So you can quote from the very best of them."

"I'm trying to impress."

"Two apprentice poet/tough guys eating Chinese food on a late evening in Manhattan, huh?"

He thought, Fine, that might just as well sum it up. It was late and he was simply enjoying this banter for the hell of it. He couldn't recall the last time he'd connected quite this way with someone.

"Tough? I don't think so. I happen to be your basic everyday pedant who has managed to fall through all the right cracks. Otherwise I'd be in Tehran right now translating general dynamics and differential equations chapters for tedious college textbooks."

During the next few days, when he had a lot of time to himself to reflect on it, he concluded that those last words of his had finally allowed her to let her guard down, though he wasn't sure why. She turned on the stereo set in the living room to a mellow jazz station. Maybe those detached horn sounds created the essential neutral backdrop so she could open up. Because she did just that. They talked until way past dawn, and she told him about the "life," as she called it. A trip to Europe that had turned into an extended stay, as she worked her way slowly eastward while the Balkan civil war got uglier. Paris first, then Berlin, and finally, muddling her way to Sarajevo.

"Did you ever make it to Sarajevo?" she asked.

"The Office was just picking me up around the time it was about to get hot over there. I never made it. Maybe I was lucky. I know of a couple of people who were there, though."

"Iranians?"

"Yeah. But they were from the legit intelligence crowd. Those people have their hands all over Bosnia right now."

She grew silent. It could have been the distant silence of someone who had seen too much of death. Under different circumstances he might have tried to set her straight, telling her that Bosnia was just another ugly page among many. In Tehran alone there were guys who had done time in the Afghan killing fields, guys who had literally crawled back from Chechnya, guys who had seen from up close the butchery done to the Kurds. And this was only the immediate neighborhood. Take the rest of the world and very quickly you'd be losing count of it all.

Yet, here was this American girl dwelling on her own sad Sarajevo experience. Did she think throwing in her lot with the Moslem cause would somehow absolve her of feeling guilt for being born in the better one-fifth of the world?

"That was where the Colonel picked you up, wasn't it?" he asked her. "I'm pretty sure he was in Sarajevo around that time."

She looked up at him with a faraway gaze. "I was doing what I could to help out. Raising money for the hospital there, trying to run a kitchen. All that stuff. I thought I was the American with the *real* lowdown on what was happening. The one who didn't come just for a day or a week or a month and then return to the States to write a book and give interviews about the horrors of war. You're right, he found me over there. Your people were the only ones doing anything real. It may have been for all the wrong reasons, but I didn't mind that. I don't mind it now."

They were both silent for a while. So far she hadn't mentioned a word about the Pakistani, Nur. Sami was cautious; he still couldn't shed the notion that even now she had planted this heart-to-heart on him for a purpose.

He said, "So our man in New York is actually a woman. And an American besides. In the Office we have a name for someone like you: *Gasoline Premium.*"

She yawned as she got up from the kitchen table. "The pay's all right, but mostly it's a good excuse to live by myself."

Sami looked at his watch. It was nearly eight in the morning. They'd been at it for hours and hours. Twenty minutes later when she came and stood by his door he was still tossing and turning in bed looking for sleep to come.

She said, "It's a bitch when you've got to make the first move."

He got up without saying a word and walked toward her. She didn't stir. He wrapped his two hands around her body and brought her close gently, the soft of her skin tingling under the touch of his fingers. She may have come to him tonight, this morning rather, for a lot more than that, but for the time being he was content to communicate the relief they shared, for he knew exactly what she'd meant by "The pay's all right, but mostly it's a good excuse to live by myself."

"You know what?" she whispered.

"What?"

"I think Havelock and Musavi are bluffing. They probably didn't kill those guys."

"It doesn't matter either way," he whispered back. "But how would you know about that anyway?"

"Oh come on!" She began to kiss him on the earlobe. "I'm your man in New York, remember? I think the Colonel and Havelock had it planned that way from the very beginning."

He took her chin in his hand and looked questioningly into her eyes. "All that just to get Zaheri over here?"

She nodded. They began to kiss, hesitantly at first, like explorers. Later when she had pulled him deep inside her on her own bed, he had a momentary vision of that Arab boy in front of the Eiffel Tower. In truth it was an intimacy he was already jealous of. He stopped to look at her. Her eyes were shut and he thought she'd whispered something in another language. Then he penetrated her again, slowly, working himself into a familiar rhythm and trying not to think of what was to come.

9

THE LOCKSMITH on 96th Street wouldn't let him inside his shop. The heavyset Hispanic man was telling Sami he didn't like to repeat himself, that he'd either have to call a twenty-four-hour locksmith or come back in the morning. He was closing up.

Sami flashed five twenty-dollar bills from behind the window. "I'll give you this besides the cost of the job."

"Fifty more."

"Fine."

He didn't waste any time. Once inside he stuck the muzzle of the pistol in the man's face and made his demand.

"All I want to know is where you keep your lock-pick sets."

"Why you mess with me, man?"

He made an involuntary move to push the pistol away from his face. Sami hooked the butt over the top and brought it nearly full force on the man's nose. The locksmith made a snorting sound and fell down. He seemed sufficiently dense that Sami could see him trying to wrestle for a semiautomatic before he gave up any part of his tool set. Reluctantly he brought a foot down on the locksmith's head. Then another, and another, until the man melted onto the floor as if he were practicing water acrobatics on dry ground.

Quickly Sami pulled the shades down and locked the door. He tied up the locksmith with the phone cord and ransacked everything until he found what he wanted underneath an open toolbox. He took all three sets as an extra precaution, one lock gun that seemed a cross between a heavy-duty stapler and Scotch tape roller, an electric pick that looked like a toothbrush, and a set of manual picks that resembled high-tech dental picks. He'd never used these things himself but had seen Mozart and others play around with them back in Tehran.

From down on the floor the locksmith was calling him an asshole.

"Sorry, friend, but you can't order these things from the catalog."

"Go fuck yourself."

"I will."

He got back to Damadi's building just as it was getting fully dark. To his surprise, the front door to the building was wide open and the doorman wasn't around. Just to be on the safe side he quickly pulled out his picks one by one and tried them on the open door. The electric pick opened this one almost as quickly as the key itself. He took the stairs up to the third floor. The hallway was empty. Hallways in New York, thank God, always seemed to be empty. If this had been Tehran a hundred pairs of eyes would have seen him entering the building by now. He fiddled for what seemed like minutes on Damadi's door. He had to make a little noise wiggling the manual picks. The electric pick and the gun were useless on the top lock. He could hear the elevator opening one floor above. A pair of voices said good-bye to each other. He was sweating now, dreading that he'd find Zaheri and his Section Nineteen shooters already waiting for him on the other side of the door.

Clever. What Damadi had done was to break a key in the lock on purpose. Sami used the key puller to get it out and then turned the lock with the double-ended pick. In his haste he'd completely forgotten to draw his pistol. But there was no one inside. In fact, the apartment was almost empty. All those rugs, the silver pieces, and chinaware were gone. Damadi had probably shipped them elsewhere or already had them sold.

He had no idea whether this was where Zaheri would show up. But if he did, it would be because he still hadn't managed to put two and two together. From the Office's deliberate leak he'd be under the impression that it was his American competitor Havelock who had been pulling all the strings against Section Nineteen. Still, Zaheri's coming here was a fifty-fifty chance, if that. But it was all that Sami had to go on. Besides, if there was one man who might be able to shed some light on how much real danger this character Nur posed, it would be Zaheri. For the time being everything seemed to ride on Sami's catching the man and making him talk.

He thought, I'm going to give this place a week. What a thought: a week of sitting on my behind in this empty apartment waiting for the chief of Section Nineteen to show up!

He might need an hour to get it together, buy some supplies, maybe a little radio and a couple of books to pass the time. Why that had to take him back to Ellena's place he didn't know. But he went there anyway, missing her, and yet half hoping she wouldn't be there at all.

She opened the door on him as soon as he put the key in the lock. There was a moment's lack of recognition. She had on a black Cleopatra wig, a wasp-waisted corset, a black miniskirt, and a pair of red leather stiletto shoes. Her lipstick, thickly laid on, looked like charcoal.

"You look like a slut."

She didn't even give him a chance to savor his sentence but slapped him so hard that his head rang from ear to ear. He must have looked dazed from the slap, because she turned remorseful. She pulled him inside the apartment and closed the door. Then she went down on her knees and started to unzip his fly.

He grabbed her hands. She looked up. "What?"

"It's not necessary. I don't need my prick sucked to feel okay."

She stood up. "I was going to say I missed you when I saw you again."

"You don't even know me."

She shook her head and started to walk away from him. "You're a fucking asshole."

She wasn't the first person who'd called him that today.

He grabbed her hand from behind. "Hey: 'Her days bent / An instrument.' Someone who can quote your own poetry can't be all that bad."

She smiled, despite herself.

"Listen," he continued seriously, "it's a screwed-up world out there, right? You said it yourself: Bosnia last year, Rwanda this year, and so on and so on. And still, who knows if I'm not fooling you right now, trying to act like Mr. Sincere. Who knows if *you're* not trying to do the same thing to me by slapping me first and then undoing my fly. And who knows if somebody higher up—if you catch my drift—doesn't have an agenda that neither you nor I know anything about."

"What's the point of all this stuff you're telling me, Sami?"

"I don't know. I guess a woman like you would have to be pretty nutty in the head to dress like this and work for my people at the same time."

"Your people, is it?"

"Don't kid yourself, don't think that ultimately you, me, even the Colonel and Zaheri aren't on the payroll of some joker with a fat numbered account in Switzerland and a house on the Riviera."

"I can see you're one to really promote your intelligence service."

"Fuck my intelligence service. My own government pays me to *watch* my intelligence service. For all I know someone's being paid to watch me. Maybe you. Anyway, I don't see what any of this has to do with you dressing like this."

"I'm going to my other job."

"You're not a whore, are you?"

She laughed. "No. I'm an entertainer. I hire myself out to parties and dance clubs. Like I told you before, it's a real job. A *real job.* It pays well and leaves me a lot of time for the other work. My mother made a similar living thirty years ago. Must be in the genes somehow."

"Tell me about your mother."

She shook her head. "Not that you couldn't find out if you wanted to. But I like to follow the secrecy rules."

"Is that why you keep connecting the dots for me but leave the big picture out?"

"Say what?"

"Like Sarajevo and all that. You have no trouble telling me about something as important as that. At the same time I don't even know your full name. It's a little strange, that's all."

"No it's not. My Sarajevo background is necessary for our rapport, yours and mine. But you don't need to know whether my daddy tried to rape me when I was a kid or if I have a brother who lives in an ashram in India."

"But it's all right for me to know your mother was a stripper thirty years ago?"

"Maybe I wasn't telling you the truth."

"Maybe you could also tell me not the truth about everything else. I'd be satisfied with that."

"I wouldn't."

"So why exactly this outfit tonight?"

"I'm a black widow spider tonight."

"It's a hell of a way to go from trying to raise money for a Sarajevo hospital to this."

"Not really. In Sarajevo the most meaningful thing I could have done was to help the hospital. In New York the most meaningful thing I can think of doing with my time is just this sort of thing."

"Sounds like poetry to me."

"It is. I call it reaching to the heart of the matter. If I could split myself into ten different people, I'd be even happier. Sarajevo was an experience, so is being a stripper in New York. Experience teaches you detachment."

"I don't see how you could get to the heart of anything through detachment."

"That's because you haven't loved before."

"I'm sorry?"

"Forget it, you wouldn't understand."

"No, I want to know."

"You have to lose the thing you've loved to really come to appreciate detachment. Have you ever loved, Sami? Has anything ever been that important to you?"

He thought about it. "It will sound incredible, but the answer is no. I've never loved. Nothing has ever been that important to me."

"It's not incredible at all. It only means you've lived a more sheltered life than I have. Don't laugh. It's true. I don't mean to make it sound like a raw deal having grown up in America. It's the best deal in town, actually. But it does have its drawbacks. A glut of choices, for one thing. People like me don't do very well with that one. We end up wanting to try everything and in the process get damaged too many times."

He was silent.

"What are you thinking?"

"Detachment. I'm trying to get a feel for what you've just told me."

"Come and watch me tonight. It might help you understand better. Or it might not. Anyway, you can always leave if you get sick of it."

He thought, Why not? Until the other week he had never sat on a bar stool to get drunk. He'd lived a vicarious life through videos of American movies. He had translated other people's memoirs. He'd learned to speak the right lingo, but in the end, that was *all* he had done. If Ellena was right and experience was the name of the game, then he must certainly be in the right company these days. He'd go. He'd go and watch her do her show tonight.

"Don't worry," she said, "don't try to read some meaning into every little detail. Enjoy the action."

Then she disappeared. He found himself standing in the middle of a low-lit three-room basement club in the Far West Village, an area where six-foot-tall transvestites paraded in high heels over cobblestone walks and young fetishists popped in and out of unlikely entrances.

Okay, something new. If she was trying to shock him, then she was succeeding magnificently. Just then a lonely looking fuzzy-faced older pervert wearing nothing but a silver ring on his penis passed by carrying a video camera. Sami thought, It's true, I'll never get used to this stuff.

The beat of the music was heavy and elemental. It was still too early. But because it was some sort of an anniversary theme night, hard-core-looking regulars were already starting to file in through the doors. Two very tall, slim-legged women wearing matching yellow bikinis and fishnet capes appeared on a side platform and began practicing high kicks to the techno sound. Then a group of well-built young Hispanic men wearing similar black polyester shirts and tight white pants came through and immediately took the middle of the dance floor for themselves. Within forty-five minutes the crowd had doubled, but there was still a lot of room for more. By eleven o'clock, Gothic-looking youngsters with pale faces and sickly makeup had claimed their own corners. More transvestites came in. A giant screen showed film footage of Marlon Brando looking oddly Japanese and singing a song. S&M couples showed up one at a time, like rare species on special display, leashed to one another, the women showing bare breasts, and the men's butt cheeks pushing through the cut leather. You had to ask yourself if these people ever got cold—if they ever wondered where World War I got its start or argued over who was the greatest boxer of the century.

She had given him a half-pint bottle of Smirnoff. "Hold on to it and drink in case you start to lose your nerve." He'd heeded her advice and was slowly starting to loosen up. At some point he looked up and noticed that some sort of webbing had been thrown across a small part of the ceiling. A man and a woman pretended to make love over the net. The crowd cheered them on. The man sprayed a whitish foam over the woman and then started to lick it. That made the crowd watching from a few feet below go wild.

The woman was Ellena. It took him some time to see that through all the netting above, but when he finally did he felt as if somebody had punched him hard in the stomach. Then without thinking twice about it he walked over and pushed a stranger off the chair he'd been dancing on. He pulled the chair to right underneath Ellena and her partner and climbed on top of it. Next he reached over and yanked hard on the man's hair through the netting, making him sink far enough so that their faces were a breath apart.

"It's tough, but if you don't quit this shit act right now, I'll gouge your stupid eyes out."

He didn't have time to witness the response. Before he could even turn to Ellena, someone had kicked the chair from under his feet and he was crashing down. When he got up he saw that four guys wearing baggy suits and wraparound shades had surrounded him. They were the security for the place and he'd noticed them kicking a drunken guy out earlier in the evening. Now they all converged on Sami at the same time.

He looked up, he looked to the side, and then he drew Havelock's H&K semiautomatic and pointed it at the one nearest to him. No one challenged him on that. He stepped backwards a few paces and then casually walked out.

He took a cab uptown to her place to pick up essentials. On the way back he bought a little food and was inside Damadi's apartment an hour past midnight.

10

THE NEXT DAY it snowed hard. The bare apartment was cold. He realized the gas hadn't been turned off, so he moved everything into the kitchen and spent a lot of his time warming his hands over the blue flames of the stove and listening to a jazz station with the volume turned low on the small radio he'd picked up. The kitchen was off the entrance passage, which meant he'd have the clear advantage if they made straight for the living room. But if they didn't, he knew he'd have to shoot his way out of that space and ask questions afterward.

The second night, as he was listening to an American broadcast of the BBC news, he jumped when he heard footsteps crossing the hallway. It wasn't the footsteps that had startled him, but the realization of the ridiculous mistake he'd made in not sticking the broken key back into the top lock. On his hands and knees he crawled over every inch of the dark apartment during the rest of the night looking for the piece. It would have been easier to go out and get another metal piece to stick inside there. But he was already feeling spooked and had decided he wouldn't leave the apartment until a full week had gone by.

With daylight he managed to find the broken key piece. It was lying on the carpet near the door right where he had first started his search seven hours ago. Exhausted and cold, he turned the stove up only to watch the last of the flame give out at the touch of his hand. He lay on the icy floor and slept for a long time. Anybody could have walked in on him then. But no one did. When he woke up again it was already getting to be dusk outside.

He was losing track of more than just time. You entered a zone that defied the infamous *cold* people mentioned far too often. The Colonel had drilled it into their heads: "Remember, we don't have any Natan Sharanskys to trade for you if you get caught. You are on your own out there." Out of all the dumb things he had done in the past few days, any one of which should have gotten him picked up, the dumbest had been to forget that the Americans usually assumed that *operative* and *terrorist* were synonymous terms—unless you happened to be a member of the Golden Shit Club, a generic name people at the Office used for any of the Western intelligence services, including the Russians and the Israelis.

By the morning of the third day he was glad to be running out of the abominable bologna and cheese he'd brought with him, and he had a serious need for some good strong coffee. He stuck it out until early afternoon and then began getting restless. The walls were closing in. Outside, snow had come and gone and the streets had turned foul. He thought of his apartment back in Tehran. He missed it only because it was his. But he also missed waking up early to go stand in the bread line by the bakery near his block. Things of that sort.

Inevitably he gave in to daydreams, imagining Ellena taking the young Arab's picture in front of the Eiffel Tower. Ellena in Sarajevo. The Colonel smoking his pipe. The Colonel in Sarajevo smoking his pipe and making a pitch to Ellena. Why in the world would he want to make a pitch to an American woman in the first place?

This time the footsteps halted in front of the apartment. He pricked up his ears. Quickly turning off the radio, he made sure the kitchen door was open to the exact distance it had been before. He was sure there was more than one person out there but couldn't tell if they were three or four or even more. Someone wiggled the broken key out of the top lock. Then there was a squeak and the voices entered the room. They were three.

Zaheri had that searching, vaguely sincere look of a conquering Western hero's Middle Eastern sidekick. With those deep-socketed eyes of his and his naturally watchful demeanor he could have easily been cast for a role alongside Lawrence of Arabia. But all this belied the fact that he was Section Nineteen's undisputed boss. He ran that department's semiofficial paramilitary camp in northern Tehran with an iron fist. His power derived more from his connections outside of Iran than from inside, which was why his enemies left him alone. In the past ten years any number of fledgling terrorist organizations—from such disparate groups as the Lebanese Hizbollah, the Kashmiri JKLF, the Armenian ASALA, and the Abu Sayyaf faction from the Philippines—had come and gone through his camp. From inside Iran he usually handpicked candidates from the MOIS people and ran them through a severe vetting process. But with Sami he hadn't done that. In fact, Zaheri had only met with Sami briefly once and then only to ask him pointed questions regarding some Bosnian trainees, which Sami didn't know anything about. The Byzantine world of Iranian intelligence being what it was, these questions should have alerted Sami that Nineteen's head had just thrown him a false feed to take back to the Office. Why? He didn't know, except maybe to gauge the depth of the Office's penetration into his own hallowed camp. But the bait that Sami hadn't taken then had come back to haunt him now. Zaheri, it seemed, had been on to the Office from the very beginning. This was looking more and more like a test of strength between two rival services that didn't appear to be so clandestine to each other after all.

Sami stepped out of the kitchen and let the three intruders hear the sound of the pistol's slide being pulled. The man standing beside Zaheri turned quickly and went to draw his own gun. He was moving so fast that the only option left was to shoot him before he returned the favor. The silencer made the bullet's flash sound like a strong thud. It was a clean shot right through the forehead; as the man went down, it appeared as if somebody had just dotted him with a Brahman sign. Damadi was next. Sami hadn't planned to go about it like this. But Damadi gave him no choice. He backed away from Sami toward the stationary Zaheri, crying a pathetic and rather loud "*No!*" several times while trying to find shelter behind Zaheri's back. When Zaheri pushed him away in disgust he made right for the window. It was a risky shot to take, but Sami took it anyway. He put a quick knee to the floor to avoid the window and shot him in the hollow of the back. Damadi froze for a fraction of a second the way B movie actors do when they get shot in films made in Bombay and Hong Kong. His cry was a gurgle that got lost in his throat. His knees sank and he went down.

"Back off. Turn around." Sami was pointing the gun at Zaheri now. "Put your hands over your head." Damadi was squirming in pain on the floor. The sound of that heavy thud once again; he put one more slug in the back of Damadi's neck and the fellow stopped moving. "Turn around." He frisked Zaheri. No gun. He checked out the other man. "Who the hell is he?" Zaheri started to turn around. "Stay as you are. What's his name? Is this the infamous Nur everyone's talking about?"

Zaheri shrugged. "Saleh. I think his name is Saleh."

"You think? Where did he come from?"

"What do you care? A bodyguard. A Bahraini Shiite. What is it you want, Mr. Amir?"

That was the million-dollar question. He wasn't sure what he wanted. His job was to kill this man, plain and simple. But what he really wanted were some answers.

He asked sarcastically, "Now you're getting Arabs to do your killing for you?"

"I always have," Zaheri said irritably.

"All right, then, since we are talking on the level here, maybe you could tell me what this is all about."

"Mr. Amir, there's a lot you don't understand. You're way over your head in this. Now, I won't deny you were going to be eliminated, but that's only because you were in the line of fire."

"Look who's talking."

"No hard feelings, Mr. Amir."

"You don't get off that easily. Start talking. Start by telling me about Joe Havelock or whatever his real name is. The American, the one you've come here for."

Zaheri remained silent.

"He's in competition with you, isn't he? Old business partners gone their separate ways. Am I right? You really have to be an idiot to want to plant bombs here to get your people elected in Tehran."

"There wasn't going to be a bomb. It was all a setup. I thought you would have figured that out by now."

"I did. To have me get caught here and blame the Office for it over there. To have an excuse to tear us to pieces. Is that it?"

"That's a fair conclusion, I'd say."

"But you never counted on the Arabs taking this game more seriously than you. This Pakistani ghost, Nur—you have no control over him, do you? Whose payroll is he on anyway? What if he brings the Brooklyn Bridge down tomorrow? Were you guys going to plant that one on me and the Office, too?"

"Another brilliant assessment."

Sami put the safety back on the gun and stood there looking at the back of Zaheri's neck. Sweat was dripping off Zaheri despite the freezing apartment.

"You guys really make me sick," he said, more to himself rather than the other man. "Every one of you—you, the Colonel . . ."

Zaheri stomped his foot on the floor in genuine anger. "Your Colonel is a traitor."

"What?" Sami came closer until he was almost breathing on Zaheri's back. "Don't try that psychological crap on me."

Zaheri began slowly this time, as if he were dictating a difficult sentence to a first grader. "The Colonel . . ."

The door burst open then, with Ellena moving through it like a lead member of a SWAT detail. She held the revolver up straight at Zaheri. Sami tried to put himself between the two of them, reaching his hands out in a desperate plea to keep her from shooting.

"Stop. I've already got him."

"Move, Sami!"

He dropped to the floor a millisecond before the clumsily silenced gun sent a bullet exploding into Zaheri's face.

He could only watch as she coolly stepped over him, went up to the prostrate Zaheri, and put another bullet into his skull. Then she stepped over Sami again, made sure the door was firmly shut, and stood looking unperturbed at the carnage in the apartment.

"We have to get out of here right now," she said in a ghostly voice.

Sami was still staring at her in disbelief. Finally he got up to take a closer look at Zaheri's dead body.

"What in god's name did you kill him for?"

"It was our job to eliminate him."

"It was *my* job," he almost shouted.

"Take it easy, Sami."

"I don't want to take it easy. Who the fuck are you anyway? I don't know you from Adam. Where did you come from? What does an American woman who has perverted fucks lick whipped cream off her body in public have to do with Iranian intelligence in the first place?"

"You're showing your true colors, Sami. Maybe you should have gone to theological school instead."

He shook his head. "Fuck you. You think I bought that bullshit story about Sarajevo? For all I know, you could be CIA working to send me on a one-way ticket to the nuthouse."

"You've been watching too many movies."

"Damn right I have. Trouble is, too many of those movies have a grain of truth to them. And it's that grain of truth that's making my ulcer bleed right now."

"Too bad. We have to get out of here *now.*" She turned to open the door.

He grabbed her. "Not so fast. Tell me something—that picture of the Arab boy in front of the Eiffel Tower in your drawer, is he another one of your casualties? Was he a traitor, too? Did the grim reaper give it to him from the back while you were busy fucking him from the bottom up?"

She slapped him. It was the second time she'd done that, but it stung just as bad.

He felt like his voice was cracking, but he controlled himself and continued. "Or was it just that you missed out on all the fun of the terrorist decades and you wanted to make it up fast? The fucking Cold War came and went and poor little Ellena was left stranded in Europe with no one from the Action Direct people or the Red Brigade coming to titillate her soul."

"Are you finished now?"

"I had a few question I needed to ask him," he said with a resigned, almost pathetic voice.

"He was a traitor."

"How do you know?"

"How does anyone know anything? I was told. I had my orders. You had yours."

She waited while he went around the apartment dusting off all the places he thought he might have touched. That took far too much time. A minute later she came up to him and said, "We have to put a light to them."

"Jesus, what?"

"Three John Does with no records in the States. The apartment is probably under an assumed name."

She was right, of course. But how could he get himself to do it? While he was standing there in a daze, she went in and came out of the kitchen carrying a meat cleaver she'd found.

"Listen"—she handed him the cleaver—"do the next best thing. Their fingers. I can't do it."

He took it and threw it away. "No!"

She made as if to fetch it. He drew his gun on her.

"You fucking sap," she cursed, "they were thugs—killers. You think I like any of this?"

He didn't move.

"Okay, have it your way."

By now too much time had passed already. With a piece of cloth he went through the pockets of all three bodies and cleaned them out. As he did so he thought distractedly about far-off scenarios: Interpol, dental records, the effect of Zaheri's death in Tehran politics if and when it should become known. Meanwhile she just stood there. A minute ago she had looked genuinely disgusted with him for being so weak. But now she looked sympathetic, as if what he had to go through was beyond his own understanding, but at least *she* understood.

She'd done his job for him. And by doing so she'd let loose a hurricane of questions in his head, more than ever before. As they got ready to open the door to leave, she held him back for a second. Then she reached up and kissed him.

"This is for the slap?"

"No."

He wasn't mad anymore. In truth he was feeling a capricious tenderness all of a sudden, as if they'd just completed some sort of atonement instead of killing three men in cold blood.

She whispered, "Let's go."

"Okay," he said, knowing the questions would return to hound him before morning, and he'd have to approach them with a different tack than he'd showed until now. "Let's get out of here."

11

SHE DIDN'T GO TO WORK that night. She was making a pot of tea for the two of them in the kitchen when he came and stood by the door.

"What?"

"I've got to get out of this country."

"Three airports serve the New York metropolitan area. Take your pick."

He was seething again, losing control. He felt like hitting her right now.

"You don't seem to understand, or you pretend not to. American justice doesn't give a damn about the fine shades of difference in Middle Eastern politics, especially when it comes to dead bodies on its own soil."

"Send them a note, then," she said distractedly. "Put the whole thing down as a favor to them. They'll understand."

"Understand what? You think they'll be any more sympathetic when I explain how, in point of fact, I saved their federal police force a whole lot of man hours by getting rid of Zaheri?"

She turned to face him.

"We!"

"We what?"

"You're forgetting I pulled that last trigger. If anyone ought to be getting nervous right now, it's me. And, hey, I don't have the luxury of catching an airplane to another part of the world like you do."

"So why *aren't* you getting nervous?"

"Who said I wasn't?"

"Then why don't you quit the bullshit talk and come clean for once?"

"It's not exactly my cup of tea, this coming clean *for once*. But all right, Sami, state your goddamned case. Go on!"

She, too, was growing louder now, and it was starting to feel as if he were arguing with his wife over when they should trim the lawn.

He asked pointblank, "Whose side is this man Nur supposed to be on?" He looked carefully at her profile to see her reaction when he mentioned the Pakistani bomb maker's name. But either she really didn't know or was just too good at this farce; she didn't bat an eye. Her reaction, or lack of it, made him even more incensed. He wanted to hit her with something juicy. What came out of his mouth instead was utterly puerile. "Then correct me if I'm wrong: you also didn't happen to be fucking the Colonel on the day Nur's name came up."

She was quiet for a long time. Then speaking in a hushed

and sober tone, she changed the subject altogether. "Listen, you'll have plenty of time for your low blows. As far as what happened today in Damadi's place, all you have there are three bodies with no connections to anyone. None. Jesus, you're supposed to be trained not to get spooked like this."

She'd changed the topic too easily. It was the first time he'd actually caught her in the act of running circles around him. And yet her underestimation of him was his best card. Not only did she know about Nur, but there had to be more to Ellena herself. He'd have to remind himself to look at things with a sharper lens from now on. In any case, two could play the game of putting a blind in front of a blind. Now he wanted to do a switch on her switch and see if it would force her to break down. A sadistic act, almost.

He kept watching her for a while. Then in a quiet voice he asked, "This isn't the first time you've killed someone, is it?"

The teapot she'd been holding in her hand went flying against the sink and smashed around them. Then she was screaming at him.

"It is. It was. What do you want from me? Why don't you go get your orders from your boss?"

And now she was crying. She was weeping uncontrollably in front of him and he didn't know if this was just another act on her part or if she was genuinely losing it as he was.

The joy in their voices was wholly unfamiliar to him. In two separate cubicles two men, one Pakistani and one West Indian, were busy speaking to the families they had left behind in their respective countries. He waited his turn to use one of the telephones in the twenty-four-hour long-distance-calling place on Lexington Avenue.

It was risky making the call from here. But it was even riskier to call Farmani in Tehran and give him a public telephone number in the States that he might not be able to get through to. Farmani, Sami knew, was the kind of man who interpreted small mistakes as signs of weakness, and he equated weakness with danger, danger to himself.

The Indian owner of the place assured Sami there was no trouble in receiving a call here, as long as he gave a time frame and was charged a base twenty-dollar fee whether he received the call or not. Sami decided he could live with that. Tehran was eight and a half hours ahead of New York City, which made it almost noon over there right now. He already knew Farmani wouldn't like him calling. If anything, the old man would try to sound more upset than he really was in order to avoid being asked for favors.

"Hello."

"Hello, uncle, I'm calling from New York. New York City."

The hesitation in the other's response was far shorter than Sami had expected. Did he happen to know something? Farmani spoke in what was probably the most avuncular voice he could muster.

"Are you all right, kid? Is New York City treating you well?"

Thankfully, he hadn't missed a beat. In Sami's experience old counterintelligence men were seasoned scumbags who managed to transcend themselves on a daily basis.

"Well, actually, I'm running kind of low on funds here, uncle. Tuition is high at school and I don't have a work permit yet."

"This call must be costing you a fortune. Let me call you back."

Sami said, "Are you sure?" Because it was the right thing to say. Then after Farmani had taken his number they talked their way around to an agreed time between the next hour and twenty minutes past that.

Sami paid the Indian the cost of the call plus the charge for keeping a line open between 5:00 and 5:20 A.M. The only thing he could do now was to go for a walk. He turned one way first, then another, to put as much distance as he could between himself and Damadi's apartment. But he realized that to walk about with nothing better to do than to fret over whether Farmani was going to call or not would drive him mad. He saw an all-night diner and went in to order coffee and a hot cereal.

You could always backpedal or even disappear, he thought—disappear into the great American underbelly and never come out. Catch a plane to Los Angeles and get an under-the-table job working for one of the many crooked Iranian gas station owners, doing the graveyard shift for a year or two before moving on. Men on assignments abroad often had such thoughts. A few ended up acting on the impulse. Most didn't. But almost all asked themselves the question at least once during their careers.

He wondered if Farmani had ever put the same question to himself with quite as much urgency as Sami was doing right now. Farmani, the old-timer with an instinct for the comfortable life. But comfort for Farmani could not have meant amassing riches. Could it? Otherwise he wouldn't be living in Tehran right now. The idea was to reduce the risk by playing the percentages—a game that Farmani must have mastered long ago. He'd been a Savak counterintelligence operative for its domestic department since the agency's inception—or at least since after the CIA/MI6-backed coup of 1953 that had returned the Iranian king from exile. His dossier wasn't exactly thick, but it was substantial enough to show he'd flourished in his own small way throughout those years. By the end of 1979 men with Farmani's background had one of two choices: get out of the country before the revolutionary mobs hung them from construction cranes, or cooperate with the new bosses in the hope that they'd be forgiven. The second group had of course never made it past 1980. And the first group—the guys who'd managed to leave the country? What had most of them to look forward to but lives of drudgery abroad, punching 7-Eleven store cash registers in Los Angeles or pumping gas in the outskirts of D.C., hoping for the bad dream to end soon? Guys like Farmani had been the foot soldiers of their time, just as Sami was now. They didn't have a secure telephone line to the American White House, nor were they on a first-name basis with a Kissinger, a Brzezinski, or a Richard Helms. At best they were a rung or two above the poor jerk who sat inside his newspaper kiosk opposite the Soviet embassy in Tehran and was given a monthly pittance to watch the special license plates coming in and going out. At some point Farmani must have looked hard around him and realized that what was coming could only be bad. He'd begun to obliterate his own records. How he did it was *his* secret and Sami had never pretended he wanted to wrest that information out of him. But the disappearing act was a thorough enough job that only through a fluke, when the Office had been ransacking a hitherto undiscovered storage space of the old *Special Office of Information*—a sort of free-floating intelligence-gathering bank of the old regime's making—had

Sami come across Farmani's name. The Office wasn't out to hang any old Savak agents, but only to knock on their doors—if they still happened to be around—and say the stock "Hello" and to see if they might serve as potential assets in some form.

Turned out Farmani was one of a handful of old-timers still alive and in the vicinity. So Sami had decided to keep this one for himself. And why shouldn't he? Instead of passing on Farmani's dossier to the Colonel, he'd simply walked out with it. A few days later he was at the old man's door with a speech in mind.

"I figured I owed it to both of us to connect through the ages."

It was bullshit talk and the old man had said as much.

"Bullshit! But do come in." And they'd gone from there.

By 5:16, back at the calling place, Sami's anxiety had given way to outright fear. Maybe Farmani had decided not to call, after all. He thought about ringing Farmani's place again, but he knew if the old man had chosen to let him drift, then his phone line would be cut off by now. Sami's eyes caught the stare of the owner of the place. The Indian was looking at him with a mixture of pity and curiosity. In the next booth a Haitian cab driver was speaking a mile a minute into the speaker. The watch showed 5:18; the phone finally rang.

"Sorry," Farmani began, "it took a while to get things going."

"I understand. Can we talk?"

"The line is safe from my end. But don't ever call me again like that. Not for anything. I won't respond."

"All right, then. I'm only going to ask you this just once. You can refuse to answer if you like or you can play dumb.

I'll hang up and won't bother you ever again. I didn't threaten to give you up the first time I came to your door and I'm not going to now."

"You're preaching, Sami. What is it?"

"I've been preaching too much lately, it seems." He was quiet for a few seconds, then said, "I won't ask who your employer is, but . . . I need a reference in the States. I need a contact who can answer some questions."

These weren't easy words to put to someone from a distance of so many thousands of miles. He gave Farmani time, knowing that the old man had a lot to sort through in the space of a few seconds before he could come up with a response. Farmani had to weigh the risk of not answering at all, despite the reassurance Sami had just given him. And yet, if he did answer, he would just about be admitting that during all those years of devoted counterintelligence work for the Savak, he had already been on a second government's payroll.

To nudge him along a little Sami added, "It really wasn't that hard to figure out. Who could get rid of their records so cleanly unless they had outside help?"

Outside help only meant one thing: the Americans, the ones who had set up the Savak's entire infrastructure and even oversaw a number of its bureaus for a long time from the inside. Yet it was safer not to say this outright. Farmani needed the reassuring lie that Sami believed he could have been working for *any one* of these organizations: the CIA, MI6, the Mossad—all of which had run officially sanctioned joint operations with the Savak before the revolution in Iran.

"Do you know what the MESA conference is?" Farmani asked. His tone of voice was like that of a man who had been suffering from a sixty-day-old flu.

"It's the annual conference of Middle East scholars, I think. Why?"

"You're in luck. This year it's being held in Columbia University. Columbia University is . . ."

"In New York." Sami had already realized where Farmani was going with this and he was getting impatient for a name.

Farmani said, "The name is . . . Fateh. Professor Fateh."

"How do I know he'll be there and if there is only one Fateh?"

"He'll be there."

"Thanks a lot."

"We are even now, Mr. Amir."

"No. I owe you big-time."

He could tell Farmani didn't want to get cut off just yet. But to hang on now, even for a few more seconds, would mean that information would be flowing the other way round.

Softly he hung up the telephone.

By the time he got back to Ellena's apartment it was six in the morning. He watched her for a while as she lay sleeping in her room. On her desk drawer a fresh piece of paper had been torn from the notebook.

"A room that negates satisfaction," she'd written.

The meaning, he thought, fell deaf to his ear. Either that or he was simply too preoccupied to consider poetry right now.

She was lying on her stomach with her body curled into a question mark. A container of compressed whipped cream—probably the same one she had used for her black widow spider show—sat on the floor near the clothes closet. He picked it up, shook it, and squeezed a little over his own wrist. Then he tasted it slightly with his tongue. It lacked sweetness. When he turned to leave he saw that her eyes were open and she was watching him.

"What time is it?" she asked.

"Late. Actually . . . early."

She reached out to him. "I'm sorry."

He kept his eyes on her but didn't move.

"Why?"

"Come here."

He went and sat next to her on the bed. But when she tried to embrace him he flinched and shook her off.

"You don't trust me, do you?" she said.

"It's not my business to trust or distrust you. I take my orders. Last I heard we were supposed to be working on the same side. Unless something has changed since then."

"Nothing has changed."

"Very well, then."

"What will you do now?"

"Go back I suppose," he said halfheartedly. But just as he said this he realized he was passively forging his own emotions for the sake of the job. He hadn't meant what he'd said at all.

She reached out to him again. He didn't move away this time.

"Maybe you could stick around for a while."

He allowed himself a dull smile. "I don't know. Either the scales are too big in this country or I'm just too small. Think I'd fare better if I was a Russian or something."

"I'll tell you what it is: you're repulsed. You want to leave Sodom to its satanic ways and go home. I'd like to know what happened to you the other night at the club?"

He didn't respond for a minute. "I felt outrage," he said

finally. "It came over me in a flash. I wanted to kill the guy licking whipped cream off your body."

"Is that why you're afraid of touching me now?"

"Maybe," he said, almost apologetically, "maybe I feel you're just a little bit tainted."

"Of course, I forgot. You may be half American, but you were raised on the other side."

12

THE OFFICE FINALLY had an affirmative on Nur. "He must be getting his logistics together," was how the Colonel put it. "It's a matter of time before he comes around." The next best dates for a catastrophe in New York, Sami figured, were either Christmas or New Year's Eve. It was the middle of December now. The Pakistani had between one and two more weeks to figure out who had deliberately botched things up for him in New York. Unless he had intelligence on the Office itself, he'd be blaming Section Nineteen for the disappearance of his unwitting cohorts Abdul-Karim, Zuheir, and Hazrat. On the other hand, his finding out that the head of Section Nineteen himself, Zaheri, had been assassinated in New York would immediately sharpen his senses. This was a gamble that the Office and Sami were prepared to take. On the bright side, however, they could also count on Nur not taking anything for granted. If he had any sense at all, he'd be wary of his own backers, the Libyans. He'd want to do a little research back in Tripoli on Musavi. And having done so, he'd quickly realize that Musavi was not at all who he claimed to be. This would divide his attention from the start and he'd be convinced he was going to have to give battle on two fronts.

The weakest link in this line of reasoning was that the Office was relying too much on the acumen of an adversary, thus betting on the fact that *because* of his sharp intelligence Nur would come up with all the wrong conclusions. What nobody at the Office wanted to acknowledge was the worst-case scenario: what if Nur correctly concluded that his supposed backers from both sides, the Libyan Musavi and the Iranians, had joined forces for whatever reasons of their own? How would the Pakistani bomb maker react then? Would he pack his bags and go back home for now? Or would he be driven even more intensely to put his blast of a signature to it all?

For Sami, the waiting game was now in full swing.

On top of this Ellena had taken to following him. The weather was clear and cold most days, and the latest flurry of snow had already frozen into a solid layer of ice on all the side streets in Ellena's neighborhood. The two of them maintained a silent sort of truce most of the time, a queer Christmassy lull that isolated them from the throngs of tourists all about the city. Sami had read the papers diligently for any word about the murders at Damadi's place. The *New York Times* had reported nothing at all. And even the more crime-oriented *Post* seemed oddly unimpressed by the idea of a triple killing. There had been a short, general report but nothing more. No conjectures. No hints that the police were following up on any clues. To Sami it appeared as if someone on the other side was working overtime to keep a lid on things. He wondered about Joe Havelock again and the possibility that the man might be more than he seemed. He could always call that telephone number Havelock and Musavi had given him. But he didn't want to make the commitment unless he had something more concrete to go on. In the meantime, he was sure they'd find him if they felt the need.

The MESA conference Farmani had leaked to him was due to start on the eighteenth of December and run for three days. It was an odd time of the year for a conference of Middle Eastern scholars, but there it was. And Sami had to wait for it to come around. Otherwise he'd have to fly all the way to Salt Lake City and the University of Utah to get to the man whose name Farmani had mentioned. And even then, how could he be sure he had located the right Dr. Fateh out of all the catalogs he'd browsed through at the New York Public Library on universities that offered Middle Eastern studies programs? The list wasn't very long, but how was he to know that the fellow didn't teach in a history department, or sociology, or even literature? And calling Farmani for more details would be useless, too, at this point, because the old man was bound not to be answering his phone for a while.

So Sami bided his time. He hung around Columbia University a couple of days to get his bearings and to find out where the conference was due to take place. It was here that he noticed Ellena following him. He didn't mention this to her, though he was nearly certain she already knew that he'd noticed her. It was an odd game of one-upmanship that neither of them could put out in the open. What they did instead when they came together at the end of those few days was to make love, quietly. This, too, was part of the truce, as if an edge lay in silence that neither wished to put aside.

One night, however, she told him about the Arab in the photograph by the Eiffel Tower. Had she taken that picture? Yes, she volunteered. In 1990. And he'd guessed right, he *was* an Arab boy, a dead Algerian who had declared his undying love for her four months prior to getting taken out by the French GIGN. Her tone switched from intimate to one of slight vehemence as she related her story. As if she was out to prove to him that she, too, had earned her marks the hard way in this business.

He said, "Hey, you don't have to justify yourself to me. I come from the other side, remember?"

"Yes, but you don't believe in what you do. You collect a paycheck. You even take pride in mentioning that."

"Would you rather have me pray to Allah too many times a day? Would you rather I vow to kill all filthy unbelievers to the last man? Tell me something, have you ever been to the Middle East?"

She had to think before answering. "It was felt I shouldn't."

"Of course. The Colonel thinks of everything. But let me tell you this, if you ever did go there, you would change your tune in a minute."

"How do you know what my tune is?"

"I've seen your type before."

"Oh, you have, have you?"

"I don't want to fight."

"I want to hear," she insisted.

"Okay . . . I call it the Florence Nightingale syndrome, with a few major adjustments, of course."

"Of course!"

"You want to get your feet wet. That's about the gist of it. It's not enough for you to know there are Ethiopians and Congolese dying in deepest, darkest Africa or wherever. You want to go down there and stuff vitamin C down those poor bastards' throats. You want to help your Algerian lover in front of the Eiffel Tower throw off his French yoke, except you forget that the French haven't a thing to do with why those idiots are butchering each other in Algeria right now. What I'm telling you is God's truth."

"What's your point, Sami?"

"The world is a real ugly place, is my point. If you were in Sarajevo as you say you were, then you *must* know exactly what I'm talking about."

"So what is it you suggest I do? Would it please you more if I moved to West Palm Beach, Florida, tomorrow to practice my golf strokes for the next ten years?"

"No. You know that's not what I'm saying either. Except that the guy who plays golf in West Palm Beach every day might, just might, be less inclined to do evil than a whole lot of supposedly well-intentioned people."

"All right, then tell me this: What are *you* doing here?"

"I'm here to prevent a mess from happening. I'm here to keep unnecessary triggers from being pulled. I'm here to keep alarm clocks that kill people from going off. I'm here for that sort of thing because that's what the Office does."

"Fair enough. But let's say you'd been picked up by Section Nineteen instead of the Office at the very, very beginning. Let's say it was Zaheri who had picked you out as one of his instead of the Colonel—would you not have tried to do your job just as you are doing now?"

He had to think about that one. Finally the only answer he could give was to try to bypass the question altogether.

"You're absolutely right."

"Answer me."

"Ellena, we talk at cross-purposes. I'm saying you have the choice that I don't have. I was born over there, raised over there. I have a passport from over there. But you—for all I know, your ancestor might have been one of the Founding Fathers; your parents might even own a beautiful golf course somewhere down in Florida. Who knows, maybe that's the real reason why you're here in the first place, a rebel without a bloody cause."

"Sami."

"What?"

"If you really want that background file on me, all you have to do is ask."

"Has mine helped yours?"

That was a smack. Not exactly calculated, true. Nevertheless, he had known how it would be perceived when he'd said it.

She was silent for a while. Then she said, "We make choices, Sami. Sometimes we stumble into something and then we confirm *that* as a choice. You and I, we're both stumblers. In that respect we're not very different, so don't pretend we are."

He looked at her and began to smile. Then he whispered, "Birds of a feather, right?"

"Something like that. Right."

MESA—the Middle Eastern Scholars Association—Sami decided after the first day of its gathering, was a mixed bag of graduate students, professors, and Middle East watchers, all of whom made a living from and got substantial mileage out of being *knowledgeable* about a messy part of the world. The lectures were held in different locations on the Columbia campus in upper Manhattan. Of the professors, a good one-half of them he knew by sight, especially the ones who had written on the contemporary politics of the Middle East. Some of them had even come to Tehran to give lectures. Professor Fateh turned out to be one of these. Sami felt stupid, not having realized it before. But in the past few years the Office had saddled him with so much written material to either translate or synopsize that he had completely forgotten he'd actually read one of the man's books, one that ostensibly had something to do with power in the Middle East. If the book wasn't about anything more specific, it wasn't because the writer hadn't known exactly what he was doing. Sami had said as much in his written report to the Domestic desk. He was used to such books and articles by now. The gist of what they usually said was to rehash and repeat bunk scholarship so as to safely conclude that things would get worse in such and such a place or they would continue as they were. Intelligence analysts, especially from the Western services, often paid lip service to the idea of not falling for this oldest trick in the book. And yet—to the benefit of their lesser opponents around the globe who could little afford too much analysis—they fell for it anyway. They did so because it was easy and because it made everybody happy.

So there he was at last, Sami thought. Dr. Fateh, your typical go-to guy regarding things Middle Eastern. He'd have a teaching position in a well-respected American university, he'd have the American State Department consulting him regarding his speciality; in the meantime the doors would still be open to him to go to Iran, pretend to do research, and even end up hobnobbing with Islamic Republic officials just because he happened to have written a book on a subject that was obvious to anyone who bothered to read the newspapers.

But Sami's interest in Fateh went a shade deeper still. There was, he recalled, that interview Fateh had given to the English edition of *Tehran Times* in early 1993, where he had interspersed praise with careful criticism to such an extent that Sami had begun to have doubts right than and there if the fellow wasn't on assignment out of Langley, Virginia. Such suspicions became second nature after a while and you learned to pay attention to them, in the same manner that you learned to pay closer attention to people who were too nice.

Now Professor Fateh stood on the podium in the half-empty auditorium, a lanky man in his fifties with a shiny bald head and a dull incurious gaze that made one guess he knew just about everything there was to know about Saudi Arabian oil output during the Gulf War or the latest purchases of heavy artillery by the Syrian military, but not much of anything else. And here, he was part of an incongruous cast of characters that included Ellena, the Colonel, Zaheri, and Sami himself—not to mention Havelock and Musavi and probably a whole network of other government vultures from various countries whom Sami had no idea about.

Sami had taken to carrying a college-student backpack and wearing a pair of round gold-rimmed glasses around the Columbia campus. He fit in. Even now, sitting in this auditorium, no one would have taken him for anything but a slightly overage political science student with a keen interest in Middle Eastern politics.

Professor Fateh's lecture meandered through a list of various names of public figures who had a chance of rising above the crowd in the coming parliamentary elections in Iran. After he was done, a question-and-answer session lasted for about fifteen minutes. Afterward the crowd began to thin out. Sami waited by the outside steps to the auditorium so as to have a clear view if Fateh decided to leave the building from the other side.

It was past six o'clock and already dark. The temperature was well below freezing. He watched the ghostly silhouettes of the few remaining college students on campus as they walked mostly alone or in pairs, trying to stay one step ahead of the cold and not saying much of anything to each other. A small crowd was still lingering in the lobby of the building Sami had just come out of. He could see them under the light, exchanging notes and picking up information about upcoming lectures the following day. They looked to be mostly Americans and Persians, with a good number of Arabs and Israelis among them. Fateh was there, too, surrounded by a student group asking him questions.

Shivering from the cold, he waited it out, puzzled as to why these people even bothered about the Middle East. What fascination drove them to come all the way here to attend a lecture less than a week before Christmas about parliamentary elections in some godforsaken part of the world like that?

"For the same reasons as you!"

Truth was, it was a thought that had been forming in his head for a long time and now he'd actually whispered it out loud. For what was any of this but another means of making a living—no different really than performing open-heart surgery or collecting garbage at night.

When Professor Fateh finally came out of the building, he had two other men accompanying him. All three were Iranian and he could hear them speaking Persian among themselves. Sami followed from a reasonable distance to the main entrance gate of the campus on the Broadway side. At that point one of the two men who had joined Fateh parted company and turned north on foot. Fateh and the second man crossed the street and hailed a cab going downtown. Traffic, even this far up, was still fairly heavy. He knew he had to act fast not to lose them. The light turned red and all the cabs stopped on the other side of the intersection. In the meantime a lone brown livery cab turned into Broadway from the side street and came to a halt at Sami's foot.

"Follow that cab."

The African cab driver grinned, displaying a set of ivory white teeth.

"You got to be kidding, man."

"Follow that fucking cab." He threw a twenty-dollar note on the driver's lap. "Stay right behind them. Don't worry about being seen. Nobody is going to notice you."

The drive seemed interminable. And the driver muttered enough times about it not being worth his while to go so far downtown in a livery cab that Sami finally threw him another ten into the bargain. At 67th and Central Park West the other man got out of the cab, but Fateh continued on. They rounded Columbus Circle and turned into Central Park South. After the turnoff into Fifth Avenue the traffic came to a crawl. Then just as the driver was about to open his mouth again Professor Fateh got out of the yellow cab.

"Thanks!"

The sidewalk was busy enough that he could easily stay

close to his man. Fateh ambled down Fifth Avenue at a leisurely pace, stopping to look at store window displays. He looped around Rockefeller Center to watch the ice skaters and then returned to Fifth Avenue. Sami kept no further than ten feet from him the whole time. On 48th Street, Fateh finally turned right. The crowds suddenly dwindled to a few lone individuals and Sami had to be more cautious. He guessed Fateh was staying at one of the hotels in Midtown and was probably heading there right now.

He was right. There were four luxury hotels on the block they were walking on. Fateh stopped and walked up the steps of the most unassuming of the lot, on the north side of the street. This was the only point where it could get hairy, Sami thought. He could play it safe and content himself with finding out where his man was staying for the time being, or he could go for it within the next few minutes. On impulse he decided to do the latter, not knowing how long Fateh was staying in town and if he'd have another opportunity to do this again.

He was lucky: a large Oriental family was just about to check into the hotel; the small lobby wouldn't be empty. Sami lingered close by the lobby telephone with his back turned to the desk. He heard Fateh ask for the key to room 801. There were two elevators. He couldn't really take the risk of having Fateh notice him from the lecture. Which meant he had eight floors to run up as fast as he could. He eyeballed the area and headed straight for the stairway. Then he ran like he had never run before.

By the time he got to the eighth floor he thought his heart was going to pop out of his mouth. A maid passed by him and went into a room without giving him any notice. For all he knew, Fateh could have already gotten here and entered his room, thus making things more difficult but not impossible. He heard an elevator ding two floors below and then after what seemed like a very long time he heard another ding. This time the elevator door opened to the eighth floor and Fateh walked out. He was alone and walking in the opposite direction from where Sami was standing. From the configuration of numbers, room 801 had to be one door from the last. Sami started to tiptoe fast. And just as Professor Fateh was pulling on the door handle to go inside, Sami reached beside him and gave him a violent shove into the room.

He slammed the door shut, drew the gun, and made a display of putting on its suppressor.

Professor Fateh was lying on the floor with his back against the front of the bed. His arms were outstretched in an attitude of crucifixion and he had a look of utter terror in his face.

"What—what the hell is going on here?"

"Shut up!" Sami continued to play the uninterested heavy for the time being.

"Here"—Fateh began emptying his pockets of all their contents—"take anything you want. Credit cards, cash, I'll even walk to the bank machine with you if you want."

Sami finished with the pistol and looked over at Fateh. He walked up to the terrified professor and knelt down so that they were face-to-face.

"I don't want the bank machine," he hissed.

"Then what do you want from me?" Fateh continued, terror-stricken.

Sami pulled back. He sat on the bed and regarded the other man for a while. Slowly he raised the muzzle of the pistol so it was pointing at the professor's face.

Fateh began foaming at the mouth. "I beg you, tell me . . . what you want. I . . ."

"Professor, you're finished. I'll shoot you first and then I'll take your cash and credit cards anyway. How's that?" he said in Persian.

Hearing Persian spoken, the professor's level of fear reached a higher plateau. He stared at Sami for a long time, as if he was catching up to an old guilt he had put away long time ago.

"What is this about?"

"You're finished. Your game is finished."

Here Sami faltered a little bit, though the professor was too afraid yet to notice it. Truth was, he hadn't quite figured out what he was after and what he would glean by cornering this particular animal. Now face-to-face with his catch, he tried to locate a hook the professor would bite on.

"I assure you I have no game with anyone," the professor began to say.

Sami raised his free arm as if he was going to backhand the other man but then let it drop on the way down. The professor cringed and covered his face. Some men feared the thought of physical pain more than pain itself. Sami could see the professor was not trained not to break. Yet at the same time he was a player, but for whom and to what extent?

He gambled on the only generality he thought he could get away with at this point. "You've already been tried in absentia in Tehran. You're a traitor. There's nothing you could tell us that we don't already know."

The professor asked, "Who are you working for?"

The question, its audacity under the circumstances, took

Sami by surprise. He eyed the professor. "Who do you think I'm working for?"

"If you were working for Iranian intelligence, I'd be dead by now. It's not their style to hang around like this."

Sami blurted out, "Zaheri is dead."

The professor's eyes widened for a second. Then he said, "My dear boy, there's no surprise in that." He was gaining his composure now. He started to get up off the floor but Sami raised his pistol again.

"Tell me about Section Nineteen."

"Nineteen is getting ambushed and good riddance. Now, if you'd been sent here by Nineteen, I'd have had a bullet in my head for saying that already. Am I correct?"

"Don't bet on it."

"What do you want from me, young man?"

"Who's setting Nineteen up? And who killed Zaheri?"

"A nice bluff, that second question. You killed Zaheri, of course, since no one in Tehran is sure about it as of yet. As for who has set Nineteen up, that would have to be the infamous Office—*the Office,* shall we say?"

Professor Fateh was smiling now, the same smile in fact that he'd been feeding his audience during the lecture. Sami stood up from the bed. He turned away from him, then turned back around and smashed the butt of the pistol over the other man's left shoulder. The professor let out a moan as if he was ready to pass out. Sami raised his hand a second time. The motion was enough.

"Please, don't hurt me again," Fateh begged in Persian.

"Who are you working for, asshole? Give it to me straight or you're a dead man in the next two seconds."

"What difference does it make? We're on the same side, aren't we? We're trying to put an end to Section Nineteen."

This time Sami smashed the pistol against the professor's left jaw, not violently but hard enough to bring tears to the man's eyes.

"Just nod once if I'm on the right track. Now then, you're working for the CIA."

The professor nodded.

"You've been a plant at least since 1993 when you gave that bullshit interview in the *Tehran Times,* if not before."

The professor nodded again.

Now Sami raised the pistol and held it under the man's nose. "Okay—the CIA has a very serious contact in Tehran. Say yes or no."

"Yes."

"That serious contact happens to be the Office. Yes or no?"

"Yes."

"The Office and the Agency are cooperating to bring down the hard-line elements in Tehran, starting with Section Nineteen."

The professor nodded his head.

"Yes or no? Answer my question."

"Yes. Yes goddamn it, yes."

"Then how come I didn't know about it?"

"Who the hell are you?" Fateh cried. "You're nothing. You, whoever *you* are, were sent out on a job. To set up Zaheri and kill him, no doubt. It was not necessary for you to know that it was a cooperative effort. It was too sensitive. Can't you see that? But no, of course not; you have to start getting big ideas into your head and come looking for me. God knows how you found me, and I don't want to know, to tell you the truth. But

I'm telling you this, kid, in case no one else has told you yet: your job is finished here. You've completed what you were sent here to do. Now you can go back home and pick up your laurels."

"That's what you think," Sami muttered under his breath, thinking of Nur.

"Pardon?"

"Nothing. Sorry about the damage, Professor."

Fateh, the corner of his mouth bleeding and his face drenched in sweat, got up with difficulty from the floor and started to pour himself a cup of water from a flask by the dresser.

"It wasn't personal, is that it?"

Sami couldn't resist: "It was, actually."

Back on 48th Street it took him a few minutes just to get his head straight. He felt stung to the core, though not because he'd been sent drifting so far out, but rather because such intricate layers of duplicity seemed so ordinary in retrospect. He would have liked to break the Colonel's back for keeping him in the dark so long. But he also realized that the Colonel was only doing his job and doing it well. And in any case, if things went smoothly according to this crazy scheme, then all the right people stood to gain from eliminating the hard-liners and Section Nineteen in Tehran. The Americans would get the foothold they so badly wanted in Tehran, with the Office as the connective link that held together much of their HUMINT gathering capability in the Gulf area. It would be the sort of accomplishment that the CIA could quietly bask in for years and years to come vis-à-vis the Senate Select Committee on Intelligence. In one elegant stroke they'd not only be able to install themselves at the very nerve center of the Islamic Party of God union, but the Office would also keep them well informed of anything that was afoot with the satellite organizations of the Hizbollah throughout the Middle East.

He thought he understood now why the Colonel had chosen him for this assignment in the first place, for if the Office was going *American*, then they wanted to start with an American, Sami, for the job. He couldn't pretend that this idea didn't excite him. It did. But there was too much that still remained unanswered in his mind. Havelock and Musavi, for instance. They were certainly the odd men out in all of this. He couldn't figure them out. Were they with American intelligence or not? Unlikely, especially since Musavi's Arabs had seemed so genuine. For all its sophistication, American intelligence simply did not have it in them to come up with such bona fide numbers as those Libyans of Musavi's. To Sami, the two of them, Havelock and Musavi, looked more and more like freelancers, except that for once they seemed to have gotten themselves involved in someone else's web of nasty tricks.

He walked due west, slowly and thoughtfully. After twenty minutes he found himself standing on Ninth Avenue and staring through the window into the interior of the AfterBurner bar.

There was no music but the place was crowded. Joanna cut an unlovely figure at the end of the bar working on a Budweiser and talking to herself. He had planned on avoiding her, yet barely a few seconds later he found himself quite automatically taking the chair right next to the one she was sitting on. He tried to order a beer, but the man sitting on his other side nursing a pinkish drink asked if he could buy him one like his own.

"Why, what kind of a drink is that?" Sami asked.

"It's a sissy drink."

"A sissy drink?"

Two seats down a borderline-looking kid was trying to convince the bartender he was over twenty-one. The talk got ugly and the trio of girls accompanying him tried to pull him away. Sami swore he could see an Ellena look-alike eyeing the bar from outside. But he didn't have time to dwell on that; the fellow offering him the sissy drink tugged at his arm and asked rather bitchily, "What about it?"

"He's not a queer," said Joanna, who'd had her back to them until now.

"How would you know?"

"I gave him a back rub some time ago, didn't I, cowboy?" She winked at Sami.

Sami started to back away from both those beauties until he ran smack into the kid who was still arguing with the bartender. The kid was a brawny twenty-year-old with a baby face. Frustrated at not being served a drink, he grabbed at Sami's collar for bumping into him and pushed him against the bar with a powerful grip. Maybe it was the latent adrenaline of having just dealt with the professor, but without thinking twice about it Sami picked up a bottle of Miller Light sitting on the bar and brought it bottom up right under the kid's chin. There was a pop, like a plunger being released. The kid sagged beneath his own weight with glazed eyes and went down. The girls who were with him backed off. Nobody else moved, except for the character with the sissy drink, who quickly drained his glass in visible horror.

Sami stepped over the kid and very carefully made his way to the door. A man with a hard hat on said to him, "Nice move, man." And from the end of the bar Joanna shouted to him, "Hey, wait a minute." That last was a cue for Sami to start running. And he did so for a long time, down Ninth Avenue and then west on 42nd Street. Ten minutes later he was standing face-to-face with the Hudson River.

He stood by the water and watched the Jersey lights blinking on the other side. Beyond them was the rest of America, an experience that he'd probably have to defer to never. In all these years, ever since the missionary school and much later at the Office, he had seldom given serious thought about his American half, his unknown mother's side. Nor did he dwell on it now. The thought was like loose change that might drop out of his pocket once in a blue moon; he'd pick it up, look at it noncommitally, then put it back in his pocket and go about his business.

He walked and walked and walked. At one point he crossed the street where Havelock and Musavi had held him captive. The block was pitch-dark and the weather was so cold that even the homeless pair who had been sheltering there earlier had abandoned it. He peered inside the display window of the art gallery where he had met the photographer Paula and saw that the space was completely empty now. A bullet hole he hadn't noticed before had made a slight indentation into the thick window glass.

Hours later, at exactly half past midnight, he was standing in front of Ellena's door. She seemed surprised to see him when he opened it to come in.

Without looking at her he said, "I thought you'd be working this time of night."

"I will be, in a minute. Want to come?"

"Are you going to let a spider crawl on your bare breasts or put some honey on some maniac's penis tonight?"

"No."

"Then I just might accompany you."

"Where have you been?"

"Are you my wife?"

"Under the circumstances, I'm more than that."

It was dumb to talk at all. And yet he thought he had nothing to gain by not telling her.

He said, "It was an all-out ambush from the beginning. Set up by the Office with the blessing of the Americans. The Office is trying to do a lot more than just get rid of Section Nineteen. Did you know about it?"

She became thoughtful. "I didn't know Americans were involved."

"I know it's a hard sell, but it's the truth."

"How did you find out?"

"I got nasty. Tell me something, have you been following me?"

"Off and on. It's tedious work, to be honest. Let's go."

An hour later her slithering body was wrapped around a shiny metal pole in the middle of a dance stage, twisting itself round and round in perfect declining circles to the accompanying music. Inebriated business types along with groups of younger men riding the advantage of being surrounded by their friends kept up a raucous charge while motioning for her to come nearer. When she did, they stuck anything from one- to twenty-dollar bills under the belt of her high heels. During only one barely ten-minute set Sami counted at least forty dollars dished out to her from the six tables nearest to the stage.

Sami meanwhile nursed a double shot of scotch at the bar of the Tribeca strip joint. He got sulky after a while and didn't even bother to pay attention when she returned for a second set. A tray-carrying brunette came up to him and asked if he needed anything.

Still sulky, he muttered, "Fresh air," and went back to his drink.

The place smelled like one giant urinal where ugly people came to congregate. Maybe she did this, brought him here, just to torture him.

By 2:30 in the morning he was half drunk and had already had a twenty-minute theological discussion with the three-hundred-pound bartender who looked like a Viking warrior. Ellena came and slid next to him.

"No more drinks for this one," she joked.

The Viking said, "Your boy is all right. But he has a gripe. Keeps repeating America is too big and Manhattan is not small enough. What's he mean?"

Ellena looked at Sami, smiling. "What else does he say?"

"Put it this way, he says God's got a bet going on the suffering bunch."

She kept her eyes on him. "I'm telling you, he's a regular philosopher."

The bartender saluted them both and walked off. She was still smiling in his direction, as if waiting for him to break down and call her a slut or a cock-teaser.

"I want you to contact him," he said gloomily.

"Contact who?"

"The Colonel. Tell him I want us to meet. I don't care where and I don't care how. I have to meet him."

"Why don't you call him yourself?"

"I'm not connected like you, am I?"

"Why don't you just get on a plane and go back to Tehran, then?"

"It doesn't work like that. It *never* works like that. What's that word? Patsy, is it? That's me right now. I could go to Tehran tomorrow and right away get executed for killing one of the top officials of the MOIS. Besides, that cockroach Zaheri had people from all over the Middle East. Not just Iranians but Syrians, Lebanese, Libyans, Sudanese, Iraqis. All sorts went through his camp at one time or another. I'm a dead man anywhere outside of the United States."

"Then stay."

"Just get me the Colonel. Okay? Tell him I know he can't come all the way out here. So I'll meet him at a neutral spot: Say London, Heathrow. My transit visa is still good for over there. Tell him to set a date, a time, a corner of the airport. All I want is to clear my head a little bit."

"You realize if he does agree, it means you're in trouble? Otherwise he'd just send a message to get yourself back to Tehran if you feel like chatting."

"The thought has occurred to me. Yes."

"Will you two have one on me?" the Viking-like bartender asked.

"No, we're leaving. Thanks, Phil."

They were sitting in a yellow cab heading back uptown. She reached over and whispered to him, "You're what the book calls an 'unpredictable entity' right now. I had to follow you to make sure you didn't hurt yourself."

"Do you still have your gun?"

"How about you?"

"I should have gotten rid of it. But I haven't."

"Don't fret," she said brightly. "If as you say there was an American green light to set Zaheri up, then nobody is going to arrest you here."

The cab dropped them by the house. Once inside, Sami picked up from where she had left off.

"Except if the Americans don't want it sung in half the newspapers in the world that they are working with one Iranian intelligence organization to put the nail in the coffin of another."

"In that case you and I would be silenced by now anyway. Don't go overboard with conspiracy theories. This is not some convoluted Persian rug design. It's a lot simpler than that, really. Zaheri had to be gotten rid of, and he was. I'll contact the Colonel for you, okay? You'll see, everything is going to be all right." She kissed him tenderly on the mouth. "I always thought I should have stuck to poetry, but then I would never have met you, would I?"

"You're crazy."

"If I was ten years younger, you'd call me brilliant."

They made love in her bed until morning. This time not even once was he reminded of the picture of that Arab boy standing in front of the Eiffel Tower. Two days later, when he was heading to London on a TWA flight, he thought this one over during a brief moment of complete lucidity and concluded that in that department at least he was probably making some progress.

13

SHE HAD SAID TO HIM, "I want to give you a gift before you go."

"Why? You think I might not make it back?"

"Oh yes you will."

They'd been walking through Central Park hand in hand, the very picture of a regular young couple out on a Sunday stroll. Yet when she had tried to guide him up the steps of the Metropolitan Museum, he'd become uptight, pointing at the throngs of people by the entrance to the building.

"Come on! You'll see."

"I'll see what?"

She'd gotten them a pair of entry tags and then walked him so fast through crowded corridors full of objects and people that he'd quickly begun to dread that her so-called gift might turn out to be some outrageous public act that would unmask them and put an end to their anonymity.

But then she led him into the main hall for medieval art, where an enormous wrought-iron choir screen provided the backdrop for a Christmas tree about sixteen feet tall. Around the base of the tree a warm Nativity scene was decorated with eighteenth-century Neapolitan crèche figurines. Sami looked around him. Solemn church music was wafting through the massive Gothic vaults and beyond.

"This is my gift?"

She shook her head. "Not quite."

Then she led him another twenty or so paces to a room next to the main hall, where an early sixteenth–century limestone representation of Christ's entombment had been placed in a recess vault.

"You told my bartender," Ellena said softly, "that God lays his bets on sufferers. Look at him, how could he *not*?"

He did look at him, that limestone Jesus with four centuries of travelers' graffiti etched over his emaciated body, and the compass of the mourners' gazes blanketing his passing.

He turned to her. "You're good, Ellena. You're really good."

"What does that mean?"

"Nothing."

"Listen, last year this time I was standing here by myself. The music from that other room, then that Christmas tree . . . God here . . . and . . . suffering. All of it really. Merry Christmas, Sami."

"Merry Christmas."

"It kind of makes it all a little more graspable, doesn't it?"

"Makes what graspable?"

"Why they tear each other to pieces. I can see someone hiking a long way to meet his maker. God, Allah, whatever."

"They don't do it for God or Allah or whatever."

"Then why?"

"Most of the time it's just work. And that's all it is."

She'd turned from him, disappointed. He'd caught up with her in the next room looking at a bonneted statuette of Mary Magdalene on a side stand.

"Hey, you could retire knowing you've done your duty to the age you live in," he told her. "You've killed a full-fledged state-of-the-art terrorist; you've had a few adventures, done the rounds, and seen your share of dead bodies on the streets."

"Are we back to that argument again? I could retire and do what instead? Get a waitressing job; publish slim volumes of poetry that nobody reads; write articles now and then about the hippest night clubs in town for the New York weeklies?"

"All things considered, these are not such bad options."

"Okay, Sami. You've made your point. But I brought you here to experience something sublime. You ought to pay more attention to that. You ought to start paying more attention in general and stop dishing advice. That's *my* advice to you."

He would have made a case for himself right then, in front of the Mary Magdalene statue. But she'd sounded vexed and he thought there would be more time for that kind of talk, especially after London.

Now the Oriental stewardess with the British accent leaned over him and flashed a twenty-thousand-feet smile.

"If you would please fasten your seat belt, sir, we'll be making our descent in ten minutes."

He'd steadily been downing little bottles of Johnnie Walker

Red throughout the flight and going in circles in his head about the last words she'd said to him. God, Sarajevo, suffering—big, big words. Next time he'd tell her she was full of it; that's what he'd do. He'd ask her to honestly answer which was the more difficult to accomplish: to try and pay your bills on time, hold down a boring job day in and day out, worry about your always-dwindling bank account after eating a *slightly* expensive meal at a *slightly* expensive restaurant; or to pull out a gun, shoot a punk like Zaheri in the face, and step casually over his dead body without remorse? That's what he'd talk to her about after London. But for the time being it was London he had to worry about. London and the Colonel.

A rough-looking man with sleepy, Rocky Balboa eyes had been following him ever since Newark Airport. He was sitting four rows behind, and pretended too much interest in his magazine every time Sami walked past to get to the bathroom. He was quite obviously an American, which precluded him from belonging to Section Nineteen. And if American intel or counterintel had already put a tag on him, there wasn't a damned thing he could do about it anyway. If they hadn't, however, then apparently *somebody* found him interesting enough to follow but not interesting enough to prevent from leaving the country. In which case he had nothing to worry about. He could sit up in the sky and slowly get drunk on behalf of the Islamic Republic and play the guessing game with himself for a while longer. Had Professor Fateh told on him to his American superiors? The answer had to be no. Because if he had, then he'd also be giving away the fact that he'd confessed to Sami, a known foreign agent. Was the Colonel keeping an eye on him with Rocky here? No again. Because the Office hadn't men to spare; besides, what better way to keep an eye on an *unpredictable entity* than to have him in the worthy hands of Miss Ellena?

But who was Ellena anyway? he asked himself half in jest and half seriously as the plane began to make its descent.

London time was eight o'clock in the morning. He had to pass through an elaborate search and a long shuttle ride before he was at the main departure area. The Colonel had picked a coffee shop at a center wing of a Lufthansa terminal for the meeting. Sami went through the motions of dry-cleaning himself for his tail's sake, knowing that if he didn't do so, the tail might get suspicious over his blatant disregard of tradecraft. At the same time he made it as easy as he could for Rocky to stay behind him. He'd debated whether to tell the Colonel about the fellow, so they could determine how to map him back to his source. But now he decided not to. There would be plenty of time later to meet the fellow on his own terms.

He bought a tall mug of coffee and a *Manchester Guardian*. The Colonel had said 9:05, but he didn't show until 9:17. At that point he walked straight up to Sami's table and plumped himself down a little too demonstratively.

"They keep giving me trouble for lighting my pipe here," he said.

"Then don't light it."

"Are you kidding, boy? I've seen Moslem pilgrims going to Mecca take out their damned prayer rugs and pray right in the middle of the airport lobby here. And I can't smoke my pipe?"

"Their prayer rugs don't cause cancer in other people."

"They cause worse."

"What's happening to us, Colonel? Why haven't you recalled me?"

"Since when do you put questions to me?"

Despite what he'd been thinking, he couldn't pass up the opportunity to put this man off guard. "Is that fellow over at three o'clock—is he American intelligence?"

"Why do you say that?"

"Because he's been on my tail since Newark Airport. Because . . . I'm told the Office has teamed up with the Americans."

He could see the Colonel was surprised, though he was trying very hard not to show it.

"We'll get to all that in a minute," he said gravely, "but right now I want to know about your tail and why you haven't shaken him."

What a rare bird the Colonel was for a country like Iran! One of those indispensable agnostics that no clever *mullah* from the Islamic Republic could do without. And Sami figured that whoever had installed him in the system at the beginning must have done so with a long-term plan in mind. Maybe that long-term plan was only coming to a head now, nearly twenty years since the revolution. Maybe all the talk about elections and hard-liners was just an excuse for a whole lot more. Maybe the Americans were genuinely going out on a limb this time. Still, how much of all this really had to do with these two men sitting at this airport coffee shop table right now, two men who had more or less run into each other through an accident of fate, a draft dodger and an ex–military intelligence officer looking for someone with perfect English? For all Sami knew, maybe it really was the American CIA that had been paying his wages all these years. The Office only dealt in cash, after all. Where did all that money come from? Who kept the books? Or were there any?

Sami said, "Just forget about that man for a minute and

answer me truthfully: has the Office teamed up with the Americans now?"

The Colonel tapped just a hair too nervously on the bowl of his briar and pretended to be busy with a clog in his pipe. He appeared gaunt and tired away from his desk and his classical music. Sami had always wondered about the rumors of his having multiple wives. He couldn't imagine the man with even one.

Finally the older man looked up and offered one of his familiar I'll-be-damned-if-you-grill-me faces to Sami. "And what if we had?"

So Sami had his answer from the source itself, and because he did he became thrilled and terribly apprehensive at the same time. "But why would you confirm this information about the Americans so easily, as if you'd come all this way to tell me just that?"

The Colonel threw a barely perceptible glance at their tail across the lounge. The man was still remarkably busy with the same magazine he'd had in his hand more than ten hours earlier.

"Did that fellow ever bump into you?"

"Colonel, I'm not stupid. No."

The Colonel slid a slim yellow folder across the table to Sami.

"This is yours. I'd like you to read it on the plane back to New York City."

"In the open?"

The Colonel was smiling. "Son, what do you think is in there? State secrets? Secrets, yes. But only your own."

"I don't understand."

"You think I stuck my hands in the trash can and brought

out the first piece of garbage I could find? No. I know your psychological profile better than you know the contours of your lover's body. Ah, please don't be indignant. No time for that now. You are an American. That file in your hands says so. Not completely, mind you. But it's a start."

"Why are you doing this to me?"

"Doing what? The file explains that you have dozens of living, breathing full-blooded all-American relatives from your mother's side in the formidable state of . . ."

"Don't!"

". . . Texas."

There was silence for a while. Then Sami began quietly, "You've been setting me up all this time, haven't you? Right down to my finding out for myself about the Office and the Americans. You wanted to test me, see if I would come to you first or run around like a loose cannon selling hot news."

"And I must say you came through admirably."

"You want me to move to the States. You want me as liaison with the Americans. You want someone who is not going to have pangs of guilt about selling out the damned inglorious Islamic revolution. You want to reshuffle the whole deck of cards in Tehran."

"With the help of a few friends abroad."

Sami sat back, exhausted. His brain was whistling with all the thoughts he'd just voiced. The Colonel pushed the folder closer to Sami.

"Find your roots, son. It's what everybody is doing these days. You can be a lot more help to me on the other side."

"Is this a personal request?"

"You tell me."

The Colonel got up from the table. "On second thought, don't worry about your man over there. Actually it's good if he thinks you're heading back east. But shake him off right here and go back to New York immediately. Here." Casually he passed Sami a tiny box of Iranian *Homa* cigarettes. It was a routine Office handoff, which meant the packet was laced with something—probably an awful Russian-quality microdot. "January second, go to phone booth number five at the usual time and wait for a friend holding a copy of the *World Press Review*. Offer him a pack of cigarettes. After that we're in God's hands and the Americans'."

"I always thought God and the Americans were one and the same."

"Shut up. I'm not finished yet. You have a priority list. First off, you have to find Nur and take him out. If he succeeds the Americans will never forgive us. Us means you and me."

"Are you sure this Nur business is not another one of your fictions designed to make the Americans indebted to us?"

"The Americans know nothing about Nur. If they did, they'd be going berserk right now. Find him, kill him. And make some noise when you do it; we want our friends in the New World to know how much effort is being expended on their behalf."

"Easier said than done."

"He'll come around. Word from Pakistan is he'll be making his move very soon."

"On what and whom? Me?"

"Maybe. Maybe not. What's for certain is he can't work alone. He needs backup. He also needs to know if he's being watched. Once he figures out he's not figuring anything out, he'll come to you."

"That gives me a lot of comfort. There's not exactly a whole lot of time left, you know?"

"Listen, you have to treat Nur as a tangential thing. Especially after you meet the Americans. We want them to feel we can help them with a wide variety of issues. So after you get to know our American friends a little better and they've had a chance to ingest the material we've passed on to them in that smoke, tell them this. One: aside from their military intelligence, most other intelligence they've got in Bosnia is a joke. They might look good on paper for their own silly newspapers, but they are losing the long-term game over there. The document we're passing back to them appears restricted enough that they should be able to narrow down the candidate who passed it to our side. Two: this is a goodwill gesture and there will be many more to come."

"And what am I, a messenger boy?"

"No, you're also a part of the goodwill gesture. I need someone who can go back and forth easily, with one foot in Tehran and one over there. And you don't have to worry about being seen with me or anyone from the Office. It won't mean anything to anyone. Do you understand?"

"Yes."

"There now. You could get me hanged with everything I've already told you."

"I couldn't if I tried. That's why you chose me, Colonel."

"Very good."

"One more thing. What about my contact in New York, Ellena?"

"What about her?"

"She acts oblivious when it comes to the subject of Nur. That makes me nervous. And here's a woman who knew exactly when and where I was waiting for Zaheri. She knew it better than I knew it myself. My question is, have you kept her out of this particular loop or am I not seeing the big picture?"

Now the Colonel did what Ellena had done earlier. He changed the subject. He did it clumsily, by letting his pipe drop to the table and then pretending concern over it. But Sami could see that this was a clumsy act managed on purpose, as if the Colonel was trying to slip him a piece of news with only a 50 percent chance of substantiation. The meaning was pretty clear: Ellena was, somewhat, out of the loop. What was not clear, however, was *why* she was out of the loop and whether she, for whatever reason, had initiated this herself, thus in fact shifting the burden of anxiety onto the Office.

The Colonel spoke with his head turned the other way. "Listen good, that doesn't matter. From now on we'll meet back in Tehran. But right now there's some unfinished business with Section Nineteen over there. I'll let you know and you'll let our friends know. Good-bye."

Sami felt like he had just been handed down the Ten Commandments. The Colonel walked away from him, the unlit pipe in his mouth, looking like an ambling pedophile on a stressful vacation. He'd gone on like a Bible, talking down, fusing his authority with unspoken hints that what was good for the Office was good for everybody. He'd thrown an almost seamless pitch to Sami. But did Sami believe him? Not completely. Telling the Americans, for example, that their military intelligence in Bosnia was a sieve was no small gesture. It was a challenge, and an extremely cocky one. But if it was true and Iranian intelligence had indeed managed by some divine stroke of luck to penetrate the Americans in Bosnia, the coup was so huge as to be almost beyond comprehension. It defied the laws of espionage, laws that were supposed to be the sole property of the inductees of the Golden Shit Club.

He couldn't help but wonder whether instead of being a joint CIA/Office op, this was in fact part of a new game to send the Americans chasing after their own tail in Bosnia? Was it possible, then, that the Colonel was setting him up to become an unwitting false defector? No and no. Yet you could never be a hundred percent sure.

Sami had an intense wish to be back in Ellena's apartment again, no less when he looked up to see his unflagging tail, old Rocky still nailed to his spot on the other side of the terminal lounge.

His flight back to Newark Airport departed at noon London time. That gave him about an hour and a half to lull Rocky into a false sense of mission accomplished. There was an Iran Air flight to Tehran at 11:30. He'd double back to the TWA terminal after confirming his seat for his Iran Air ticket to Tehran. So Rocky would have to be gotten rid of somewhere between Iran Air and TWA.

But then a new thought occurred to him: Rocky was the only part of the equation he hadn't considered *after* his talk with the Colonel. Who was this guy really? And why was he following him? Maybe the time had come to risk something.

He bought some odds and ends, including a book of matches, from the magazine store across the lounge. The whole time he made sure he was in clear view of Rocky so that the latter wouldn't have to change his location. Then he went into the men's room next door and quickly scribbled something on the inside of the matchbook and waited. Minutes passed. Travelers came and went. He stood in front of the mirror and let the water run again and again. After about ten minutes a very nervous Rocky showed up to see what was going on. By the time he saw Sami standing in front of the sink it was too late. He had to go over to the urinal and pretend he was taking a leak. Sami still waited. Rocky then came over to the sink next to Sami's and began washing his hands without looking up. Sami put the matchbook on the counter separating the two sinks and very deliberately pushed it towards his man.

"Take it," he sighed into the mirror. And Rocky did, just as a little boy and his father were coming out of one of the stalls.

Turned out that the TWA flight to Newark Airport had no delay. Sami was at the gate promptly an hour before to confirm his seat. He was alone. But on the matchbook he had passed on to Rocky he had written his flight number and ETA back at Newark Airport.

He had no reason to sleep peacefully on this flight, but he did. Before he went to sleep, he spent a long time staring at the yellow folder sitting on his lap. Key to his past was what the Colonel had hinted. But it didn't matter if the information in that yellow folder was true or not; what mattered was that there had been years in the distant past when he would have traded a lot for that information. Then at some point he'd changed, making it a point of principle not to be interested at all, like a frustrated bottled genie who had waited far too long to be free. Obviously the Colonel didn't know his psychological profile well enough to dig this deep. And therein lay the Colonel's own weakness: he'd rather have Sami as an American because it meant high marks to have Americans under one's supervision. At the same time he naturally assumed that Sami would welcome this with open arms, for who would pass up the opportunity to collect his pay straight from Virginia rather than have it arrive under dubious terms from Tehran? What the Colonel didn't understand and what Sami would never point out to him was that it was not necessarily more important to collect overtime pay from a winning side than just to find a simple comfortable niche somewhere. A man who had faith in psychological profiles ought to understand this, but since he didn't, there would come a time in the Colonel's career when he would have the rug pulled from under his feet from a corner he least expected. Would Sami be the one to do this? No, of course not. For one thing, Sami knew he was not the kind to rock the boat. But second and more importantly: what if deception could truly bring about an acceptable end for once? What if the Office, with the help of the Americans, managed to really pull it off this time and help install a moderate government in Tehran? This was not something totally unimaginable. Sami smiled to think of himself as a simple pawn who might help checkmate the old kingbreakers.

In any case he tucked the yellow folder into the magazine jacket of the seat in front of him without looking at its contents. Upon landing at Newark airport he'd pass on the yellow folder altogether, the same way one might pass on buying a somewhat interesting book to add to one's collection of other somewhat interesting and unread books gathering dust on the home library shelf. Only for an instant did he hesitate over the decision he'd made, thus bringing the passengers behind him who had lined up for disembarkation to a momentary standstill. He hesitated not because he wanted that folder back but because he'd been trained to be security conscious. But then he decided, probably a little too casually to make it honest, that inside were only a few names and addresses in Texas that would mean nothing to anyone who looked at the folder's contents.

In the end, he reminded himself, he'd do what the Colonel wanted of him because *he*, Sami Amir, wanted to do it and not because of a doctored yellow folder designed to make it easier for him to change his loyalties.

Then he put one step in front of the other and the line behind him started to move again.

Compared to London, his journey through customs in Newark was a breeze. He waited at the departure ramp while taxis and shuttle buses passed him by one after another. After a half hour of this he was starting to get discouraged about Rocky's level of competence. He tried to remember whether he might have failed to make his flight info quite clear on the book of matches. But no, he'd made it clear, of course he had. Reluctantly he went over to the taxi line to catch a ride into the city. A minute later a yellow NYC cab halted well behind the stop sign. The door to the driver's seat opened and Bilal, the Libyan cabbie who had chased Sami on foot around Manhattan weeks earlier and had later given him a ride to the Williamsburg mosque, got out of the seat. At that moment Sami felt as if he'd been given a special key to a lock he'd been trying to undo forever. He exited the taxi line and made toward his man.

It was one in the afternoon New Jersey time. Christmas Day.

"Thank you for accommodating us, Mr. Amir" were Joe Havelock's first words to him when they were face-to-face again.

It was an hour since he'd been picked up by Bilal. Sami

was standing in a ramshackle apartment house in East Harlem in the company of Havelock, Musavi, and the bulky Arab who had stolen his money last time around.

"But it does make me wonder," Havelock continued, "why you even took the trouble to come."

Sami looked at his surroundings. His head almost touched the ceiling of the room they were in. The only window to the place was covered with cheap and badly mangled wire mesh. He could hear the continuous sirens of ambulances arriving at the hospital across the street on Second Avenue.

"Your boy over there"—he pointed to the Arab who had to bend to avoid the ceiling—"beat me for my money last time I had the pleasure. Maybe I wanted a chance to get it back. And a free ride into the city."

Musavi looked over at the goon and said something in Arabic, to which the other only shrugged. Havelock lit a cigarette and offered Sami a broken chair.

Sami said, "You guys had me followed to London and back. I had to know who it was. That's about it, really."

"Were you guessing it was us, then?" Havelock asked.

"I wasn't sure."

Musavi came and stood in front of the chair Sami had now taken. "Who was it you saw in London?"

"The man we call the Colonel, who else?"

Musavi and Havelock looked at each other. It was a suspicion-confirming look.

Sami said, "I thought you guys already knew."

"That's not the point," Havelock said.

"Then what is?"

"That you came back to the States," Havelock answered. He'd taken over the dialogue again while Musavi contented himself with listening and keeping an eye out the window. "Why aren't you back in Tehran, Mr. Amir?"

"What makes you think I should be back there and what gives you the authority to ask?"

Havelock allowed himself a tired smile. Sami wanted to ask him if all of this ever got too repetitious, this in-and-out business of interrogating people between lunch and dinner.

"Zaheri, as you know very well, is dead, Mr. Amir. He's dead because he was in the way."

"In the way of who? You? Because he was competing with you guys in the East African arms trade?"

"Don't look so shocked, Mr. Amir. Do you really expect me to believe you were sent to New York without already knowing all this? My man told me exactly what you did in London. You wanted contact with whoever was following you, so you passed him your flight information. This suggests two things to me: either your organization is working hard to set me up or you yourself feel betrayed enough to risk everything for the sake of getting to the bottom of things."

"And which one do you believe it is?"

"It's the second one, without a doubt. Which makes the first one also true without you necessarily having anything to do with it."

If an open landscape could talk, it would talk like Havelock, Sami decided. He made half suggestions and waited for the other man to trap himself. He must have been in the business of intelligence at one point. But he was out of that game by now; the undercurrent of desperation in his attitude suggested this.

"You have me here now," Sami said, "and if I'm not mistaken, you're willing to give me the benefit of the doubt; well then, tell me straight out why you think my organization is setting you up?"

Musavi inched closer to Havelock and whispered something into the second man's ear. But Havelock pushed him away.

"Mr. Amir, I've got American surveillance on me these days. Not in the States, mind you," he was quick to point out. "Not yet. But I ask myself, why should Joe Havelock, who is always so careful, be under surveillance. Are you asking yourself this question, too, right now, Mr. Amir?"

A shrill siren came screaming through the block just then, seeming to go on forever. During this break Sami watched Musavi, who watched Havelock, who in turn watched Sami. The interminable sound of the siren made it feel like a face-off that would have to reach some conclusion by its end.

When silence came again Sami said a definitive "No! I'm not asking myself anything right now, Mr. Havelock." More silence, then he added, "Except this: just how deep *are* you with the Colonel? You don't expect me to believe you went to all this trouble to get Zaheri out of the way because he was planning to bomb New York City; you couldn't give two cents about that, really. That was just an excuse for you to cooperate with the Office on the Section Nineteen ambush. So what's your real relation with him—the Colonel, I mean?"

"Let's say we are, we *were*, business partners."

"Arms? Missile technology? Enriched uranium? Which?"

"Whichever you like to think."

"And Zaheri was trying to move in on your turf in the very lucrative Iran sector, wasn't he?"

"Something like that."

"Christ!"

"Christ has nothing to do with it. Your Colonel has betrayed me to the Americans. Why is that? Is your organization working with American intelligence now? If so, I have no trouble with that. In fact, in many ways that's excellent for business. You can take that back to the Colonel from me. Just ask him this: why is he trying to ruin me? Why has he given me away to the Americans?"

"Because you, too, are a token of his goodwill to them. What else?"

"What did you say?" Musavi barked from the window.

Sami began to repeat what he'd said, "You're a token of . . ."

At that moment the door to the apartment burst open, taking every one of them by complete surprise. Like a bat out of hell Ellena came rushing into the room with her pistol scanning. Musavi and Havelock froze. Instinctively, Sami jumped to put himself between those two and Ellena's gun sight.

"Don't!" he shouted desperately to her. "We're just talking here."

But the Arab bodyguard across from him was already going for his own gun. Sami saw that Ellena had her barrel fixed on him and the other two men by the window. Without thinking, and as if all of this were taking place in slow motion for everyone but himself, he leapt at the Arab drawing at Ellena from four feet away. The Arab became confused. He ended up pistol-whipping Sami in the ribs instead of pulling the trigger on Ellena. A millisecond later a shot smashed a low hanging lamp on the ceiling. Sami was already down and writhing in wild pain from the hit he'd taken from the Arab. He wasn't looking when a second shot came, this time from Ellena's pistol. An instant afterward when he looked behind him, the huge Arab was bleeding profusely. He'd taken a direct hit in the heart and was out of the picture for good.

Ellena came over to Sami to help him up, her gun now fixed on Havelock and Musavi, who were still not moving. She had a ferocious look on her face.

Sami got up, still doubled over. "For God's sake, put that gun away."

Havelock said, "We have to get out of here."

"Shut up," Ellena commanded, still holding the gun up.

His breathing was hard. It didn't feel like a broken rib, yet the pain was real. He looked at the dying Arab with mixed emotions, almost wanting to search through the man's pockets and retrieve the money he had stolen from him.

"You've proved more than once you can handle a gun," he muttered to her. "Now *please* put that thing away."

She did. "You okay?"

"I'm all right. How did you know I was here?"

"I followed you from the airport. I had your schedule."

Havelock and Musavi shifted uncomfortably.

Ellena asked, "What did they want from you?"

"It's a long story. I'll tell you later." Sami looked up at Havelock, coughing up blood as he tried to speak. "This was an accident. I swear to you on that. But I've heard you out. I've heard you out loud and clear."

"Question is, what are you willing to do about it?" Havelock said with regained composure, as unfazed by his goon's dying as if the man had been lying there in his own pool of blood for recreation.

Propped with difficulty on Ellena's shoulder, Sami was walking toward the door. He turned back to them. "I don't know yet. I don't know what I'm willing to do about it. You guys still have that number?"

Havelock nodded.

"Nur is on the loose," Sami coughed, realizing full well that the Colonel's supposedly immaculate compartmentalization of the subject in regard to Ellena was being chucked right out the window. "You guys help me when the time comes and in return I'll pass you advance warning about the feds here."

"Sounds like a gentlemen's agreement," said Havelock.

"It has to be."

Sami and Ellena were almost out the door.

"Mr. Amir!" Havelock called out as they were disappearing.

Sami turned around one last time. "Yeah?"

"Let's try not to kill each other. It would be a shame."

"Yeah, okay."

14

ONE OF THE TELEVISION channels had been showing a 007 marathon for the Christmas holidays. The ones Sami had already seen he saw again. Some of the ones he hadn't watched before proved unworthy of a second glance anyway. Within half a day he'd developed a nervous bedside rhythm of switching between dry firing with his pistol at points invisible on the bedroom door and watching TV. He'd surf the television channels relentlessly. After about forty hours of this he could safely conclude that Sean Connery's compassion, his almost plebeian suavity, worked wonders from one improbable scene after another, whereas Roger Moore's attempts at the same made him appear like a wet hog in a white suit.

He'd stopped coughing up blood, at least. Ellena had insisted on taking him to the emergency room, but he was adamant about not wanting to go. His ribs were still too tender, forcing him to plan out all his body movements beforehand. Slowly he was trying to pull himself out of the torpor he'd fallen into. There was the coming meeting on January 2 with the CIA handler. Meanwhile Ellena was acting mysteriously. It wasn't any one thing that she'd done that made him wary of her. It was the general way she'd carried herself so far, starting with her shooting of Zaheri and then Havelock's Arab bodyguard. During recent days, however, she puttered about in her room. Strangely, she doted on him at the same time, setting his meals by the bed and going out of her way not to demand an explanation about what had happened with Havelock until he felt up to talking. The first time they'd talked was the morning after the East Harlem incident.

"I've never been treated this well," he said about her nursing him.

"I think we ought to let a doctor look at you."

"It's not necessary."

"I'm sorry about yesterday," she said, "I thought you were in trouble."

"Maybe I am. Maybe *we* are." Then, despite himself, he let it all pour out. He started from the beginning, skipped ahead to the present, then doubled back years and years to Tehran, to how it was during the war, to his long period of waiting; he told her about the army draft board, about a man everyone knew only as the Colonel, about how he'd gotten picked up by the Office, all the books he'd translated for them, told her about what it was like to work there, how they could little afford infighting since they were always too busy charting the activities of those sleazeballs at the Interior Ministry, at Intelligence, at Military Intelligence, not to mention the Sepah, the Komiteh, and the Basij people. He told her about how he'd always wanted to see San Francisco, to stand by the ocean and look into the horizon over the Pacific. He told her about assignments in London and Paris. He returned time and again to the Colonel, about their last meeting, about a slim yellow folder the man had passed across the table to him, a folder containing the history of his American half. He told her about how he'd left that slim yellow folder in the magazine jacket of the seat in front of him on the airplane. When she'd frowned at this revelation and looked at him questioningly, he'd explained to her that, no, it wasn't because he was afraid of what he'd find in that folder, or in Texas, for that matter; it was because if the past few years at intelligence work had taught him anything, it was to be careful when an elder slipped you a map that was supposed to contain the keys to all of your mysteries.

"It's easy to draw maps," he'd told her, "and they're not always the right ones." She said nothing to that, nor did she object or even open her mouth when he confessed to her that after all that was said and done he still didn't trust her. "For all I know, you could be an Israeli plant; only *they* could pull off someone like you," he blurted during a moment of inspiration, and waited in vain for her to disagree so he could read her reaction. Then having said that, he threw caution to the wind altogether and told her about the microdot on the pack of Homa cigarettes. He told her about his new role as liaison between the Americans and the Office. He told her about the meeting he was due to have with an American handler soon, and how he wasn't sure if he ought to try, despite the Colonel's order to the contrary, to recruit their help in stopping Nur. Still she said nothing. So he passed over that and went on. He talked about how he'd gotten picked up at the airport, about a pair of desperate men, Havelock and Musavi, waiting for him in a dingy East Harlem apartment.

"You can be sure they are desperate, all right. How do you know they are as desperate as I say they are? Because if they weren't, they would have been far less tame with you for bursting in on them as you did. Those men would kill for a lot less than a deal gone bad, unless they realized they were in over their heads. And this time they are; they are way over their heads. The Colonel wants the Americans to think he's giving those two up to them as a goodwill gesture. But that's not it at all. Fact is, the Colonel—*our* beloved Colonel—wants no partners for himself in his little Middle East arms business."

"And you and me?" she asked thoughtfully.

"As you said before: two failed poets trying to get it right in the wrong trade. There's nothing else for me but to meet the Americans. Let me put it differently: I *want* to work with the Americans. It makes no difference to me if the Colonel stands to make a fortune from all this, as long as one result of what he's up to is to send all the Koran wavers packing out of the Middle East."

He watched her closely. He was sure he knew what she was thinking: so what about her? She was an American citizen who had been freelancing for an unfriendly foreign government all the while; it didn't make an iota of a difference to some gung-ho knucklehead at the FBI's counterintelligence or the U.S. Attorney's Office if she'd been doing this for a secretly pro-American segment of it. Some time ago she had said to him: *I don't have a plane to catch to another country.* Neither did he now, but with the difference that he was sent here from the east as a gift of sorts, whereas she . . . ?

He asked her, "Has he contacted you—the Colonel, I mean?"

She shook her head. Then she got up to leave. Before doing so, she turned around and kissed him for a long time. It was a desperate sort of kiss, something on the scale of a plea, and he wasn't sure how to interpret it. He tried to look into her eyes, but she turned from him again and quickly left the room. After that episode she withdrew into herself even more and left him alone.

She appeared busy, but he didn't know what she was busy about. She came and went. Spent most of her time in her own room with the door locked. When she did come to see him she had a cryptic look on her face. She would run her fingers gently over his swollen ribs and kiss them. She would feed him heated canned tomato soup that he'd asked for by spoonfuls. One time she even sat down and watched the tail end of *Dr. No* with him on television. But other than that, she seemed to have dissociated herself from their surroundings, the way probably only a dance club stripper knew how.

On the night of December 29 she left the apartment around 11:30. He was sick of James Bond. He got up and tried a push-up on the floor, feeling a horrible spasm in his chest as soon as he pressed his hands to the floor. In the kitchen he found an untouched bottle of Barbados rum in the closet next to the fridge and sat down to it. A short half hour later he was tipsy enough not to give a damn. He went to her bedroom and tried the lock. It wouldn't give, so he went and fetched the picks he'd taken from the locksmith's shop.

Once inside her room, he lifted the notebook from her writing table.

She'd written:

Something moaned
In her?
No
Though it could have been the oud she plays
When he calls for her

He decided she could do better than *moan*, but he liked the movement of the long line. It had possibilities. Also, it had an Oriental tinge. The image of a concubine maybe, languidly playing the oud. An odalisque. And who was the *he*? A sultan maybe? A grand vizier?

He stood in the middle of her room with his eyes on her desk drawers. He needed more than just a few lines of poetry. He wanted to know her life as he'd told his to her. But she hadn't made any serious offers, had she? At least nothing that went further back than Sarajevo. As if life had only begun for her from that point. And in a way maybe it had. But still, he needed to know more. He needed to know who she was, where she came from.

No sort of correspondence anywhere in her house. No letters, bills, or junk mail. Not even a name on her mailbox downstairs. He rummaged through the drawers for anything of that sort. There was a Chase bank statement addressed to a post office mailbox. Her full name: Ellena Giorgione. Italian stock? Ellena Giorgione of Italian stock with a Chase bank statement for last September letting her know she had eighteen thousand dollars in her checking account. Five withdrawals for that month. One large deposit of four thousand dollars. All of this said nothing except to add a little meat to her edges. Ellena Giorgione who wrote poems!

In another drawer he found an old Christmas card without the sender's name. "Ellena Dear," it began, "Merry Christmas." Then there was an illegible signature. Her mother maybe, Mrs. Giorgione? Who else would call her Ellena Dear? Where had Ellena Dear come from?

He was hurting again. It felt as if the booze he'd just drunk had made a hole at a point just below his sternum. He sat down on her bed, one hand gingerly holding his stomach and the other his forehead. It wasn't just the pain; he was also exhausted with himself, exhausted with his untenable attraction toward this woman. And then he began to dread again. What was going to happen to her next week or next month or next year? Was there really a Mrs. Giorgione in some place like Flushing, Queens, or Toledo, Ohio, who sent her *Dear Ellena* Christmas cards and to whom she could go back to without the specter of the man in the gray suit following her?

His foot caught a piece of wire heavily wrapped in black electrical tape. It was the sort of thing one would normally pick up only to throw in the garbage can. But this made him curious. With difficulty he bent over and ran his hand under the bed. What he came out with was a medium-sized Toshiba radio–cassette player, circa early eighties, with a large round black speaker to one side of it and a tape deck on the other. The radio band was predigital and the button system was 1970s technology. A cheap and ugly contraption that, although not ancient, would be hard to find in many Third World countries nowadays. Why had she kept it? The screws to the backboard were loose, so he started to undo them. But before he'd finished he knew exactly what he was looking at. Then his heart began to beat a lot faster and his hands started to sweat as he came to treat the Toshiba radio–cassette player with new-found respect.

At that moment Sami Amir was quite sober.

He knew where to look and what to look for: a Swiss-made demolition timer in the lower-right interior of the machine capable of 100 percent accurate delays of one to ninety-nine minutes or one to ninety-nine hours. He was no demolitions expert, his knowledge of bombs being limited to the few big hits that had been shop talk for the last fifteen or so years. Yet in recent times there had been one multiple big hit which, unless you were a blind deaf-mute you couldn't help having been lectured on: the black Toshiba radio–cassette player. The American ATF had brought one back from Togo in Africa in 1986. Its original source was guessed correctly by the Americans, and already known to the Iranians and Syrians, to be Libya. Then in 1988 the West German BKA had raided a safe house in Neuss and found almost the exact same device in the car of a senior lieutenant of the Palestinian PFLP-GC. Bombs have their signatures and no two bomb makers make any one bomb the same way. So once information had started seeping out, it had become pretty clear whose signature was on the black Toshiba: Ahmed Jibril, a former Syrian army officer and master technician now working for the PFLP-GC. It was the same sort of bomb that had brought down Pan Am flight 103 over Lockerbie, Scotland, with the exact same copy of the IC timer as the one recovered in Togo, with a barometric switch and ten ounces of Semtex-H plastic explosive.

To his relief there was no Semtex-H in the machine he was holding in his hands. No barometric switch either, of course. Delicately, he put the cassette player on the bed. He brought back a piece of cloth from the kitchen and carefully wiped off the entire machine. He screwed the backboard on the way it had been before and wiped off the back again. Then he put the whole thing under the bed where he had found it. He also dropped the piece of electrical tape and wire on the floor. When he was sure the bedroom looked exactly as he had found it, he turned the light off and relocked the door from outside.

Had his stomach not been hurting so much, he would have finished off the entire bottle of rum right there and then. Instead, he went back to his own room and lay down. He flicked on the television switch just as one of the newer James Bond heroes was taking an impossible flying leap with his motorcycle into thin air in order to catch up with a crashing two-seater airplane in some Siberian wilderness.

He turned the television off and lay quietly thinking in the darkness, though his state of mind was hardly quiet. Was Ellena Giorgione, or whatever her name was, working for Nur and the Arabs on the side? Might she be some sort of a parallel agent performing nonrelated tasks for different intelligence services? He didn't want to think so. And yet she did have the famed black Toshiba in her hands. Didn't she? Before long he was starting to spin wild scenarios in his head. He wondered if she might not have been an American counterintelligence operative from the very beginning. Since he was supposed to become a liaison with the Americans, might this be a test to see if he would report the Toshiba to his new CIA handler? No again. The Americans might do a lot of things that were not on the up-and-up, but they didn't go so far as to shoot people in cold blood, as Ellena had done with Zaheri, in their own backyard. It just wasn't done, at least not quite that way.

God knew what awaited him if he tried to retreat now and go back to Tehran. Here was another foolish thought: what if there was a way to retrieve the yellow folder the Colonel had passed on to him and move to Texas? Move to Texas with Ellena. Ellena Giorgione with a Chase checking account and an Ahmed Jibril time bomb under her bed.

Farmani was angry right away. "We agreed you wouldn't call like this," he barked instead of a greeting. Yet the old man was not hanging up on him. That in itself was *something*, though it wasn't necessarily a sign of fear or excessive favor. It was just plain old generosity—a lifetime traitor's generosity that still risked a lot on the part of its giver. So Sami in return made it easy for him by disconnecting from his own end. There wasn't much the old man could have offered him anyhow.

He'd made the call from a corner phone booth off Avenue C in the East Village, a semigentrified block with a couple of bars and an occasional dope dealer canvassing the street. The chilly wind slid right over the icy ground and hit you hard on the extremities. It was noontime. There was almost no one about, few people coming out of their holes in this neighborhood before midday. He walked down the block, went into a local Korean delicatessen, and got a large cup of coffee. When he came out again everything looked the same except for the small hatted figure who was now lurking near Avenue D on his side of the street. Sami felt watched. He'd been feeling it all morning, ever since leaving the house to go make this pointless call to Farmani. Even now he still didn't understand why he'd bothered to make the call at all.

If that man on Avenue D was a tail, then he had to be a solitary one. Still, he'd play it safe for now, especially because he hadn't seen Ellena since before last night's cassette player discovery. He walked at an unhurried pace westward toward Tompkins Square Park, restraining himself from turning to see if he was being followed. As soon as he hit the park from 10th Street he stepped up his stride and did a quick loop to the left side of the entrance so he'd be in a position to watch his man if he came up from the same side of the street.

Sure enough, the previously idling hatted figure came pacing up 10th just a little too hurriedly. This still meant nothing. It could simply be one of Havelock's men keeping an eye on him. But then again this could be Nur finally making his move.

Sami hustled back to the main pathway in the park and pretended he was trying to decide which direction to take. It was certainly not your run-of-the-mill local park, this. On a patch of grass to the side a yogi-like character dressed in an all-white outfit was staring intently at the bark of a tree. Another man walked in precise circles around both the tree and the yogi whistling Sinatra's "Strangers in the Night" to himself. Meanwhile a shriveled-looking wino crossed the path dragging a coverless guitar case on a leash.

Sami lingered a little bit to give his tail time to catch up. Then he turned down and came out from the southwestern exit of the park. He feigned a phone call on Avenue B and saw that his man was sticking behind him a block further up. He hung up the telephone and continued south. There was a small community garden around here somewhere that he'd walked past before. On 4th Street he took a right and kept an even pace going west again. At the next delicatessen he went inside and asked for another large cup of coffee, though the other one was still in his hand and he hadn't touched it. He left the old coffee behind and came back out. Two blocks later he saw the community garden. The gate was open but there was no one there. He went inside and wedged himself between some frozen shrubbery and a spiraling large-scale artwork made from bent car bumpers near the entrance. He loosened the lid from the cup and waited.

He didn't have long to wait. The footsteps halted by the entrance before taking a cautious step inside.

"Hey," Sami whispered, and by the time the hatted figure had turned to face him, the steaming cup of coffee was flying in his face.

It caught him in the upper neck area but it was enough to make him yelp in pain. He fell to his knees, holding his hands over his face. Sami tried to yank the man's neck back. It was his friend Mozart from the Office, the very same Mozart who had volunteered unasked to watch Sami's back during those uneasy first few months at the Office.

Sami felt all the steam go out of him. He let go of Mozart and stood there limply as if he was ready to cry.

"Mozart!"

Mozart continued to hold his face. "Sami," he said in Persian, "you've really fucked me up this time."

"What are you doing here? Why are you following me?" He helped Mozart up and led him to a bench.

"Office shit, Sami. They say you'd been turned. Have you? Oh God, I need ice on me."

"Let me go get you some."

"No, stay," Mozart moaned. He picked up some frozen earth and held it to his neck. "I just wanted to make sure you weren't being followed. I don't give a fuck about those idiots at the Office."

"Who told you I'd been turned, the Colonel?"

Mozart turned to him. He had a face Sami couldn't read. It had always been that way. Mozart wasn't a particularly very sophisticated operative, but he got the job done. He was an animal that burrowed deep and managed to sustain himself with what was at hand.

"Sami," he was saying, "all I want to know is, what's your game? I'm your brother, remember?"

No, he didn't remember. Mozart didn't have a brother as far as work went. Nor did Sami. In a way it was a faux pas of the trade to say something like that; it was overplaying your hand.

"I have no game," he started to say. "I'm on a job."

He didn't have time to finish. An open fist caught him right below his ear and sent him rolling backwards over the bench. He blacked out for a millisecond and a tremendous rush of pain went through his chest. As soon as he opened his eyes Mozart was standing over him holding a semiautomatic.

"I'm sorry, Sami. I take orders like everybody else."

"You bastard. The minute you get back to Tehran he's going to have you taken out the same as me."

Mozart cocked his pistol. "Wrong, brother. You told the American girl too much. She called us. She's gone crazy and threatened to spill the beans. Rule number one: make sure you're always working for the side that's going to win. In Tehran that just happens to be the Colonel and his gang right now. As for me, I'm only protecting my own interest."

"You'll kill her next?"

Mozart smiled. "We can't have some American bitch going around setting us all up, can we?"

"What has she done?"

"Come on, friend! What do you care about all that now? Close your eyes and say your *Allah Akbar*, and I'll finish it."

Voices were passing right next to the community garden without stopping. Mozart's focus tilted for a fraction of a second. From his prone position Sami pushed with the balls of his feet under the bench they'd been sitting on and sent the whole thing flying into Mozart's face. The gun dropped but Mozart himself didn't go down. Forgetting his pain, Sami leaped to his feet and head-butted Mozart in the stomach. They went crashing down on the frozen ground together. Sami was on top and Mozart was trying to choke him from the bottom. He stiffened his two thumbs and popped them hard into Mozart's eyes. This made him let go of Sami's neck.

"You son of a bitch. I'm going to kill you." Mozart took a switchblade out of his pocket and started to slash blindly, gashing Sami slightly on the side of the shoulder before violently kicking him away from himself.

Sami felt the cold of the pistol Mozart had dropped lying right under his butt, cocked and ready to shoot. He grasped it and waited. With eyes half shut and with frozen earth still clinging to his face, Mozart came at him. Sami hesitated a fraction of a second and then he shot him.

Mozart went down immediately, as if glad to get it over with. The bullet had caught him in the guts and he was making faces as if he was going to vomit.

"Oh God, Sami," he was crying, "what choice did I have? Finish me!"

Sami shook him. "All right. Listen, what about the girl?"

Mozart mumbled an address precise enough to earn him mercy. Then he keeled to his side. Sami put the gun barrel right to his friend's temple and pulled his woolen hat over it. The shot made him jerk as if he'd just been administered shock therapy.

"Rest in peace, you miserable fuck!" He stood up, less remorseful than angry. He slid the gun into Mozart's slightly open right hand and cautiously stepped out of the garden.

He took the first cab that came his way on First Avenue. Ten blocks later he got off and took another cab. Then another. Next to the Empire State Building he went and sat in a coffee shop to drink his first real cup of coffee that day. It was wonderfully rich and tasty. Mozart was dead. The Colonel was not. Slowly the anger inside him was replaced with a juvenile uncertainty that there might not be an Eden waiting for him at the end of the line, after his having shot and killed three men in the space of a couple of weeks. He looked outside at the swarming lines of vendors and pedestrians below the scaffolding under the Empire State Building, feeling as if even that world, as close as a crosswalk away, was out of his reach, too—as distant as when he had stood by the pier overlooking the Hudson River with the New Jersey skyline on the other side. America had only been a whisper and a slim yellow folder away then. Yet so far.

He ordered another cup of coffee and tried to concentrate on Ellena. The Office was gunning for both of them now. Why? Why indeed. He felt responsible for putting her over the edge by telling her too much. But what was her crime? What exactly had she said or done that called for both of them to be put on the Office's elimination list?

The lady in the theater costume shop on 14th Street assured him the beard wouldn't come off. He told her he wanted to put it on right there. It was for a New Year's party he was invited to, but in the meantime he wanted to surprise his friends at work. By the time Sami came out of the costume shop he was down to his last forty dollars.

The beard was an inspiration he wasn't sure he needed. Yet he was not going to take any chances. With a touch of nostalgia he thought how a month ago he might have taken a photograph of himself for laughs, just to show it to his good friend Mozart back in Tehran.

He walked slowly up First Avenue, gauging all the possibilities that might come up. He had his own gun, the microdot package that the Colonel had passed on to him, and one of the lock picks from his adventure at the locksmith's shop. It took him forty-five minutes to cover the distance between 14th Street and Ellena's neighborhood. At 53rd he turned quite casually into Ellena's block and continued on down the street. If there was going to be surveillance, it would not come from the Office, since they'd already sent Mozart, who would have had the best chance of taking Sami out when he wasn't looking. No, if surveillance came, it would come from the American end, the Colonel's contacts from the CIA. It would involve a minimum number of people, no more than two or three. And even though this sort of thing was supposed to be FBI detail, the Bureau wouldn't have a clue it was going on; in fact, they'd raise bloody hell if they found out, and therein lay the rub.

Nothing seemed out of the ordinary, though at this point they could be anywhere, including inside the apartment. But it was a chance he had to take; he had to find out where she was. Holding his breath, he came up to the building and slipped the outside key into the door. No one in the hallways. No sign that anything was amiss. He came to her door and listened for a long time. Then he turned the key and quietly stepped inside. He scanned for details, maybe a mislaid book or a torn page of poetry too carefully put back in its place. Nothing like that. He looked under Ellena's bed and saw that the cassette player was gone. As he was pulling back from under there to get up, he heard the click of a gun.

"Don't make a move."

For a second he was baffled with himself, as if his clumsy disguise had already turned his mind. Then lamely he mumbled, "Ellena, it's me. Sami."

He started to get up. She was looking at him, dumbfounded at first and then amused. "Sami, what the hell?"

"It's a long story. Come here." She did. He held her tightly in his arms. "What have you done with it?"

"With what?"

"Please, not now. I know what was under your bed. Don't mess around with me. We don't have time."

She tried to push him away from her but he held on. "Look at me, Ellena!"

"Shhh!" She pointed to the hallway door. Someone was playing with the outside lock.

Quickly Sami made gestures with his hand, signaling to her to go into the bathroom, close the door, and turn the shower on. While she did this, he placed himself on the other side of Ellena's bedroom door so he'd have a direct shot at his man or men as they went for the bathroom.

The lock snapped open. Only one person came through the door, a burly-looking American with thick black hair and glasses. No gun in his hands, dark gloves, and a very small leather attaché case under his arm.

Sami let the click of the gun do the speaking first. The man froze in place. "Drop the case." He didn't drop it. Without more ado Sami sneaked behind and bumped him hard on the back of his skull. The fellow went down but didn't go out. A quick body search produced a tiny Derringer for a weapon. In the briefcase there was only what looked like a highly refined Swiss army knife and a small camera. He gave the man another good bump on the head with the stock of the pistol. The fellow was an ox and only grunted instead of passing out.

He called Ellena out of the bathroom.

She was standing over him. "Who is he?"

"The man in the gray suit, I suppose."

While she went to get a cord, he looked through the man's pockets. A Treasury Department employee card. Name: Harry Maddox. They tied Harry Maddox, who probably had never seen the inside of the Treasury Department, with speaker wire and then covered his eyes and mouth.

"Take whatever you think you'll need," Sami said.

"You think they're outside?"

"No. Not on this one. I figure Harry here is reporting directly to the head of a very off-the-book task cell in his organization. Here, Harry, give this to your boss." He placed the microdot pack inside the man's briefcase and zipped it up.

"What are you doing, Sami?"

Sami continued to address Harry, who was shaky but quite conscious. "Tell him here's a token of *my* good faith. I don't know what you guys are up to, but all I want is a little peace of mind. I'll contact you as originally planned, but only if I'm sure you're not going to put me six feet under. Over and out."

"Sami, talk to me."

"Get your things and let's go," he shouted at her. "We don't have time."

She did. In the meantime he got rid of the beard and changed into another set of clothes. They went out from the back of the building past a big communal Dumpster and a courtyard. Ellena produced a key that opened the gate separating her building from the one on the 52nd Street side.

When the cab driver asked them where to, the two of them looked at each other without quite knowing what to say. Closing her eyes and leaning back into the seat of the car, Ellena said, as if by rote, "Washington Square Park, north side. Take your time."

He said, "You haven't been truthful with me."

She said, "What makes you think you're entitled to that?"

"This is not some sort of game, Ellena."

"I didn't think it was, or I wouldn't have put my butt on the line for you up in Harlem. Would I, Sami? And now . . . I would like you to make love to me. Show me what a Middle Eastern man with a good dose of Texas in him can do."

The bed was creaky and too narrow for the two of them. The hotel room itself, overlooking 20th Street and Eighth Avenue, was large, but that was all it was. The toilet sat in one corner of the room and an out-of-use bathtub in the other. The Vietnamese proprietor of the place had charged them an exorbitant seventy-five dollars a day with a three-day minimum in advance for his fleabag establishment, claiming tomorrow's being New Year's Eve as the reason.

Sami rolled over on top of her and began kissing her ears. He thought, Mozart is probably in an icebox right now and according to him I'm about to make love to all of America. He laughed.

"What's so funny?"

"I'm . . . Back home we don't just call you an adventure but a continent. A certain fellow I shot dead this morning would have gladly died a dozen more deaths just to be here with you tonight."

She wasn't interested that he'd just admitted to killing yet another man today. Rather, she raised herself up with a pillow and tried to pull him closer to her. He resisted. "Sami, I don't mind being doomed. It's sensual."

"It's dumb. And it's not poetry, if that's what you're after."

She opened her eye to look at him. "Well, it's too late for anything else. Isn't it?"

"It may be. But it doesn't hurt to try."

Beyond that, he didn't say what was on his mind. He'd had a hundred questions to ask her when they'd been riding in the cab earlier in the day. But slowly he'd come around to the idea that whatever she was about or had done or planned to do was beyond his means of interrogation. She wouldn't confide in him for the moment. From Mozart he'd already gleaned that she'd threatened to give the Office and its budding CIA connection away. To whom? To the federals and the newspapers? If that was true, then she couldn't possibly be working with Nur at the same time. Also, as things stood now, she was in the unenviable position of being a free agent, belonging to nobody and protected by nobody. What reassurance could he give her? That he'd straighten things out with the Colonel and with the Americans and then bring her back into the fold? That was bullshit. He'd be lucky if he could save his own neck after what had happened today. It didn't need a whole exchange of words and accusations to acknowledge that they were *both* stranded right now. So he decided to play her game a while longer, this game of little girl lost at sea with sharks in the offing. There was as much point to asking her why she'd threatened the Colonel as there was in asking her why she'd gone to Sarajevo: everything and nothing. And his mistake from the outset had been to try and set her straight by telling her about the Office and the CIA working together, about arms trade and crooks and liars in general. Because now she found herself a common international whore with a deadly aim instead of an avenging angel for the downtrodden of the world.

Could it be that he was completely of? That this image of her in his mind was skewed from the bottom up? He would still play her silent protector even so, a role he didn't mind at all. He would meet the American or Americans on the appointed date. At worst they'd simply off him and she'd know she had to run. Where? Anywhere. Far away. Lebanon, maybe. A woman who carried the infamous Jibril cassette player had to have more connections in the Middle East than just a tiny supersecret intelligence organization in Iran that was now out to cut her throat.

He kissed her with his eyes closed. This time when she raised herself to guide him inside her, he responded. No, he wouldn't interrogate her, not now. He'd only listen and watch. And she, perhaps she understood his thoughts better than himself. Because she volunteered nothing except herself. Which was a lot. It was a state of mostly silent make-believe where both parties pretended to be putting off decisive action while calculating against themselves. It was . . . the poet game, *her* poet game, was what it was.

15

ON THE MORNING of the last day of the year Sami Amir woke up with a bad feeling. A minute earlier he had reached across the narrow hotel bed and realized that Ellena Giorgione was not there.

Weak winter light came in through the east window from Eighth Avenue. He'd slept too long. Way too long. Already it was almost noon. He had no idea if Ellena had left only minutes or hours ago. After they'd made love last night, fatigue like a drug had overtaken him so completely that he'd drifted off immediately in that cold uncomfortable room. And now that he was awake, all he had to go on was the address that Mozart had revealed to him yesterday before receiving that final slug in the head.

It didn't feel like the end of a year but the end of the world to Sami. As if things were winding down in an unreasonable fashion and still he had to search inside him to figure it all out. The first thing he *had* to do was to make one or two calls. He'd try to reach the Colonel first, although a lingering sense of duty still prevented him from making direct contact with the Office in Tehran. All calls had to be routed through London and passed on in order to confuse the Western signals-gathering capabilities. Yet how that worked was beyond him and most probably bogus security anyway.

On the telephone, with the usual introductions over, he asked for the Colonel by his operational name and, incredibly enough, was given another London number to call in half an hour. He spent that time sitting inside a Boston Market fast-food restaurant on 23rd Street watching couples and families line up to order their quarter- and half-chicken dinners. Twenty-five minutes later he walked back out to a less-frequented subway exit of the 23rd Street station. There was a working public phone there from which he'd make his call. He thought: I'm either telephoning people or shooting them these days.

"I already have the news on Mozart" was the first thing the Colonel said on picking up the phone.

"Why?" Sami asked. It was the only thing he could bring himself to say.

"I put faith in you, boy. Not departmentally, but man to man. I gave you a meal ticket. All you had to do was make contact and be my man abroad."

"I still intend to do that, two days from now. But you sent my friend after me. You think I've betrayed you. I haven't betrayed you."

"The American girl . . ."

"I already know. She's threatened to give you up."

"You don't call that betrayal?"

"Look, what happened was, Havelock had me picked up back in New York. That was one of his men we saw in London. I guess I was never able to shake him off," he lied. "In New York they nabbed the girl and me together," he lied again. "Then Havelock rattled on about you and him having been business partners."

"That's enough!"

"All I'm saying is, I couldn't help the situation. She was there. She heard it. Havelock naturally assumed she was one of us."

"She was."

"Okay, so she was. That's until she decided she wasn't. But I had nothing to do with that. *You* pushed her on to me, *you* snared me for Havelock and Musavi, *you* set me up to become a messenger boy between you and the Americans, and now *you're* assuming I've betrayed you. Tell me something, what have I got to gain by betraying you? If you think I'd make some crazy deal with your old partner Havelock, you're way off the mark."

Everything he'd just said was true, except he didn't believe that any one of those things gave him cause to be indignant. He was merely playing another game. And this new game called for pretending to be irritated with another man's lack of faith in him. The algebra of the whole thing was something like this: He knew that the Colonel knew that *he* knew about the Colonel's arms-for-profit side business, and also that probably more than half the Colonel's efforts to hook up with the Americans had only been for the sake of facilitating his own private deals. The CIA no doubt understood this also and didn't mind it at all, as long as it gave them a window of opportunity into the domestic politics of Tehran. And why should they mind it? Why should Sami mind it, for that matter? It was this idea that he was trying to get across to the Colonel: *I don't give a damn how much there is in it for you; that part is no business of mine.*

The Colonel said, "Havelock is as good as finished. I'm not worried about him at all."

"What about me?"

"You still have time to prove your worth."

"So you still want me to make contact on January second with the Americans?"

"Yes. But we've got Nur, too, to think about. Everything's off if he succeeds. Find that crazy girl and you'll probably find Nur in the background pulling her strings. Advertising us to the world can only serve his purpose."

"What is it you want me to do?"

"You'll know what to do when you find them both."

Sami didn't say anything to that.

"It's the only way you can come back, son."

He said a mechanical "Okay" in order to have said something; anything less would have started the Colonel second-guessing himself. Then with a voice devoid of any feeling, he asked about the address Mozart had uttered before dying.

"It's where she said I should personally meet her if I don't want her to start talking to anyone who will listen about us and the Americans. That particular address—the building, I mean—a portion of it is ours. It's one of those prerevolution New York properties the Shah had bought a long time ago. The Americans had it confiscated for years. But we have it back now. And Sami, when I say it's ours, I mean *it's ours*, the Office's. So you understand the gravity of the matter. Whatever you do, don't do it in there. Take it outside."

"When?"

"Tonight. Midnight your time. Let me know when it's done."

Back inside the Boston Market he tried to eat but couldn't get anything down. At midnight what exactly was supposed to happen? The year would change; that was for certain. And a little Toshiba cassette player might bring a floor of an entire skyscraper down; that was a guess. Again, to Sami it was the things that the two of them hadn't revealed to each other that said more about where each man stood. The Colonel hadn't mentioned anything about that cassette player, which meant he really didn't know about it, for if he had, he would have taken much more drastic measures to stop Ellena. No, he simply wanted Ellena out of the way and he wanted Sami to do his dirty work, as usual—just as he'd used him to lure Zaheri to New York. You had to admit there was something graceful about the way the man's mind worked. He used the possibility of the successful completion of his own commands as leverage against other men. He didn't need to kill Sami, but only to keep him guessing. That was precisely what he'd done to his old business partner Havelock.

Yet the only person who had rebelled against this process was Ellena. She might have asked for a meeting with him, but what she was most probably after was to blow up an office registered to the Iranian government, with or without the Colonel inside it. What mattered was the act itself: to have the suddenly enlightened ATF, FBI, NYPD, and State Department reveal happily to news agencies across America how they'd discovered an infamous cassette player in the ruined remains of an Iranian government building in New York. This would neatly tie so many loose ends together, wouldn't it? The Pan Am downing and the bombing of the Berlin discotheque for starters, not to speak of countless other incidents during the 1980s that had rightly been attributed to the Libyans until now. Best of all, it would slap the handcuffs on the newly forged CIA/Iran connection, which was apparently what had galled Ellena enough to push her to the brink in the first place.

And when was all this to happen? At the stroke of midnight, at the year's end. Not only was it a bold stroke, it was a beautiful one. It was poetic and thus quite worthy of Ellena Giorgione. It was poetic and mad, completely and utterly mad.

On his way back to the hotel Sami began to make a run-through of his options. There weren't many. Find Ellena before midnight. That was about it for now. He walked past the hotel owner, who was busy conning a group of German kids into parting with three hundred dollars. Upstairs he halted outside of his room and was about to put the key inside the lock when a brainstorm hit him: Nur would seek him today. It was as plain as daylight and as inevitable as the year's change at midnight.

Sami took the safety off his gun and ran back downstairs again. 826-6585. He dialed Havelock and Musavi's number from the public phone next to the grocery store by the hotel. Three rings. He waited. Two more. Then a low voice with a thick Arab accent said, "Hello."

"Give me your boss."

It went quiet on the other side for a long time. He was sure he hadn't dialed wrong. Late, maybe, but not wrong. Could be that Musavi and Havelock had already been swept by the Americans. Which meant there would be a trace on the line.

"Who is it?" It was Musavi's voice and accent.

Sami bluffed on the dime. He hadn't even thought of what he would have to come up with until now. He said, "Nur will have to come after me today. His best shot for something spectacular is midnight tonight. I need backup."

"Why call us?"

Sami could clearly hear a guarded tone in Musavi's voice.

"The Office wants him stopped. But if he succeeds, the Colonel plans to dump the blame on you guys."

"It's awfully kind of you to be thinking about us, Mr. Amir," Havelock's voice said from a second line.

"Kindness is not my business. My job is to stop Nur; yours is to survive. Maybe we can scratch each other's backs for a time."

"Yes," Havelock said, "but that still doesn't explain very well why your people don't supply you with your own backup."

"Because I'm in love."

"The girl?"

"The very same one."

"Sounds to me you have nowhere to go either, Mr. Amir. Maybe we can become partners after all this is done."

"Let's live through it first. I'll be at the Empire Hotel at Eighth and 20th. Room number twenty-two, second floor. The latest I can stay there is ten o'clock tonight. Afterward I'll need protection for a while. At least till I get back in the good graces of my own people and . . . the Americans."

"I think this can be managed, Mr. Amir."

"You sure?"

There were two clicks. The Havelock/Musavi team had hung up, leaving him beached with an uncertain guarantee for now.

He got himself a cappuccino and then ordered a second shot on top. There was no one in the lobby of the hotel now. He walked up the stairs, turned his key in the lock, and put one foot in front of the other half expecting to be manhandled big-time. He wasn't to be disappointed. It wasn't like in the movies; these guys didn't sit back and say something like, "Take a seat, Mr. Amir; we're here to have a talk."

No. The first thing to fly off was his double shot of cappuccino. He saw it land somewhere near the toilet bowl and almost felt more anger for the lost coffee than for his own well-being. Someone gave him a shove and someone else gave him another shove from the opposite direction. He took the bullying as a matter of course. His human radar told him Nur was within touching distance.

"What do you guys want?"

He got a smack in the mouth. He'd seen it coming just in time and knew it was from Abdullah, Musavi's Libyan. For decorum's sake he made a lunge toward his adversary. Now a foot came hard on the back of his right knee and he went down. Just as he turned to face the second man from behind, a hefty backslap caught him on the jaw.

He was giddy now. Abdullah stood on one side of him and Ahmed, Musavi's other Libyan, on the other. The only catch was that Musavi was nowhere around. In his place a withered-looking little man stood in a corner of the room smoking a cigarette. He had on a pair of blindman's shades but it was clear he could see everything that was going on.

Ahmed had to steady Sami so he could stand up while Abdullah reached in and took his gun. There was no love lost with these two Libyans. You could tell they didn't like Iranians to begin with, and now they probably blamed Sami for their bombing plot going awry. But the call was Nur's and he'd made a tactical blunder by revealing right off that he had Musavi's Libyans in his back pocket, because before the interrogation even began Sami already knew that Nur had written Musavi off as a traitor. The reason he was here, then, was not necessarily to kill Sami but to find out whose side he was on.

Sami assumed a righteous attitude. "What took you so long to show up?"

Nur continued to regard him without making a move. Sami imagined that here was a man who hid behind dark glasses because his eyelashes never moved. An android with plenty of prayers to his credit. His skin was the color of wet wood. He could have been anywhere between thirty and forty-five.

"Mr. Amir," Nur finally said, his voice a curious mix of Indo-Pakistani singsong and automaton, "the head of Section Nineteen in Tehran was shot dead here in New York."

Sami waited for him to continue. But the man had stopped short. He was trying to read Sami's response. Overdoing it would be an error. Sami said, "What else is new?"

Nur nodded his head and immediately Ahmed reached around and delivered a lunging karate punch into Sami's stomach, knocking the wind clear out of him. As he doubled over to get his breath back, a hand reached behind his neck and pushed him down. This interrogation session was going to be low on finesse.

For a long, slow-moving time Ahmed and Abdullah took turns pounding him with kicks while Sami rolled about the floor. But you could tell their hearts weren't in it. Nur had said something to them in Arabic that might have been a command that they shouldn't be overzealous about it. So in the haze of pain Sami was able to calculate that Nur was still not sure about anything and he didn't want to make hasty decisions for now. The pounding of the two Libyans began to get rhythmic after a while. He thought he'd start hallucinating if something didn't give pretty soon. All he could see of Nur were his feet facing the window. It was starting to get dark outside. Four o'clock, he figured. Eight hours before midnight. Would Musavi and Havelock wait till 10:00 P.M. to stop by? Nur in the meantime acted as if he had all the time in the world to force his man to come around.

At some point Sami vomited all over the floor. The old pain in his rib was so acute now that he could barely keep himself from rolling over and passing out. The Libyans stopped hitting him. Nur came and bent over Sami, the shades still covering his eyes. He might have been a blues impersonator in some cheap South Asian bar.

"Tell me about the American girl, Brother Amir."

What could he say to make it come out right? If Nur knew Ellena, then Ellena knew Nur. Everybody was trying to find a dancing partner here and nobody knew whom to trust.

"She works with us at Section Nineteen." As he said this Sami knew the other man would never buy it. And he didn't.

"You're lying, friend. Zaheri would never have hired an American woman. Try again, Mr. Amir."

Ahmed put his foot on Sami's throat and pressed him to the floor. Abdullah took his pistol out.

"It's the truth." He had to risk something here. It was a fifty-fifty gamble to tell Nur about the Jibril cassette player bomb. If Nur already knew about its existence, then he might buy Sami's story about Ellena. "She's got a Toshiba, packed and ready to go. She's a grade-A operator. We've used her for a long time."

Nur leaned further over Sami and seemed to look hard from behind those dark glasses. Moments passed. Here was a man who sold destruction at below cost.

"Then tell us where she's going to be tomorrow night?"

A test, and a clumsy one at that. Nur wanted to know where Ellena would be *tonight*, which meant he already possessed that particular bit of information. If Sami confirmed it, then he'd be proving to them he was deep enough in the know to be on the level. The Office had been right on the money for once: Nur had turned out to be a smart man who came up with the wrong conclusions because he was just slightly too sharp.

"I know nothing about tomorrow night. But tonight she'll be at a site in Midtown. Tonight's the night."

His interrogator was finally satisfied. "Get him up and washed. Sorry about the treatment, Mr. Amir."

"I'm used to it."

Nur started walking away toward the window again. Ahmed was helping Sami up. And Abdullah was standing next to the bed when a knock came at the door. The two Arabs and Nur all drew their guns. Then Nur motioned to Sami to ask who it was. The peeved voice from the other side claimed to be the resident manager. He wanted Sami to come downstairs and pay for his room in cash or he'd call the police right away.

Sami looked at Nur, who signaled to him it was all right to go down. Sami opened the door to go, with Ahmed following behind. Nur and Abdullah stayed inside. The two of them were halfway down the hallway when the shots rang out. Sami had made himself ready by staying to Ahmed's weak side. Having paid in cash when he'd first checked in with Ellena, he'd immediately realized that this was a ruse by Havelock to find out if Sami was alone or not. He tried to elbow Ahmed as hard as he could now, but the other caught his arm in a powerful grip and twisted it around. Another rush of pain went through Sami's body. The Libyan then threw Sami against the wall and reached for his gun. Just then a shot from behind caught him in the back of the neck and he went down. Havelock stood in the hallway with his gun still pointing across.

The only thing Sami could say was, what took them so long. There were panicked voices in the downstairs lobby and from inside the other rooms. Cops would be swarming this joint in a matter of minutes. Musavi and another man popped their heads out of number 22. They, too, were still holding on to their guns.

Musavi spoke quickly, "Let's get out."

There was no time even to look inside the room. Sami felt like throwing up again. "They dead?"

"As doornails," said Havelock cheerfully. "Is there a back way from this place?" He handed Sami back his gun.

"There is." Sami had checked that earlier just in case of such an emergency. Nur dead. And so easily, too. If he didn't feel so physically wretched, he'd have kissed all three of these men right now. "There's a fire escape through the back. It'll put us on Nineteenth Street."

Sirens in the neighborhood. But no one had seen them take off except for an old man who had fallen on his face as they were running through the basement fire door.

Havelock and Musavi were both panting. The other man with them was another Arab. A big fellow, who could have been the twin brother of the goon whom Ellena had shot in East Harlem.

"Let's walk," Havelock said.

A yellow cab was going west on 19th Street. Sami hailed it. All four men got inside, with the other Arab sitting in the front.

Sami turned to his unlikely saviors. "I'll put in a good word for you guys when my time comes."

Musavi, who was sitting in the middle, appeared ill-humored. "Good words won't be enough."

"Don't get sulky on us now," Havelock said to his partner. "What is it you can do for me, Mr. Amir?"

"I can tell you to disappear for a while. Take a Tripoli vacation for now. It may not be an ideal place for vacationing, but it beats jail time. I'll definitely put in a good word for you with Langley when they ask. I'll let them know who fired the shots that took the infamous Nur out."

"So it's really true. You guys are going American."

"We all have to sometimes. It's like eating a Big Mac in Moscow or Shanghai."

The cabbie had turned south on Ninth Avenue. At 14th Street, Sami told him to stop. He opened the door and got out. A parting word was in order, but no man was in a mood to talk. Survival was a long road and at that moment none of those men, including Sami, was certain if it was going to be worth the cost.

By 10:00 P.M. the entire Times Square area of Manhattan had been sealed off for the New Year's Eve dropping of the ball at midnight. Times Square itself had been filling up with celebrants since hours earlier. They came in droves, holding onto their balloons and blowing on their paper whistles. Sixth Avenue and Broadway were closed from 38th Street all the way into the 50s. Cops stood behind the barricades and kept people from getting any nearer to Times Square. The temperature was somewhere in the low twenties with a dry cold wind blowing over the crowds.

He knew he ought to have started on this a lot earlier. But it had taken him another couple of hours to get himself straight after parting with Musavi and Havelock. He'd taken a tiny room at the YMCA on the East Side, washed up, and dozed off for a while. He was still in a lot of pain, but he felt alert and ready to push himself as much as need be until it was past midnight.

He wormed his way through the crowds on Sixth Avenue to the barricades that cut people off from going into 47th Street. He had to get to a twenty-odd story office building nearer the Sixth Avenue end of the block. Every once in a while a group of kids would be able to charm their way past the cops in order to enter Times Square proper. He knew he had one shot to do it right, otherwise he might be spending the night in an NYC paddy wagon instead of getting across to the other side. At eleven o'clock the crowds in Times Square started to go wild with cheers, counting the minutes to the new year. The throng on Sixth Avenue started to get restless. When a gang of black teenagers tried to break through the line, a half dozen cops made a beeline toward them. At that instant Sami jumped the barricade along with about thirty other people.

He walked soberly along the sidewalk until he was next to the building. He could even see the night watchman right there in front of him, though on the other side of the tall glass doors, gazing at his video cameras behind a long semicircular counter. Every few minutes he would come and stick his chin on the glass to look outside. He was a short, thickset Eastern European–looking type with a blue uniform. Sami waited because there was nothing else he could do. Chances of Ellena even being there were not very good. If she knew how to work the Semtex-H with the time device, then she would have been out of here a long time ago. Her presence was not required to blow up the building. But if she was specifically interested in the Colonel, then it was a different story. She'd be there, waiting, unable to grasp the fact that a man like the Colonel was not foolish enough to fall for the same trick he'd played on Zaheri: he'd never come; Zaheri had, but then again, Zaheri *was* a fool.

Twenty-four more minutes passed like that. The cops were finally giving up and starting to let more and more people through the barricades. The noise in Times Square was deafening. Sami watched his man come away from the counter and head for the door. But this time instead of putting his chin on the glass, he took a set of keys and slipped one of them into the lock. Sami breathed a sigh of relief. The fellow was going to smoke. He started to walk casually the other way, and just as the watchman was putting the cigarette in his mouth, Sami gave him a fast downward punch on the nose. The guy fell back with arms widespread into the door so that his stomach was open and vulnerable. Sami delivered another blow right below the navel. This time when the man doubled over, Sami grabbed his hair and pulled him quickly inside and locked the door.

He put the watchman on the floor behind the counter and began to tie him up quickly with the cord he'd brought for the occasion. He wrapped the man's eyes and mouth with his own shirt and tied his legs to the leg of one of the desks against the wall.

Eleven-thirty. He ran to the bank of elevators that served floors ten through twenty. The space that belonged to the Office was on the sixteenth, seventeenth, and eighteenth floors. He pressed for the elevator but nothing happened. From inside the building the noise of the crowds on Times Square sounded like the purr of a motorcycle engine from afar. It came and went, then grew to a crescendo and suddenly died down. Now he realized he had to have special keys to use the elevators at this time of night and there was no time to try all the ones on the night watchman's chain. He heard footsteps coming around from the next elevator bank. Staying calm, he tiptoed fast to the sign pointing to the stairway and opened the door.

He didn't want to be completely out of breath when he got up there, so he measured his paces going up. One, two, three—if eternity was anything like this, then a man had every right to despair. He could have cried when he reached the sixteenth floor and realized that the door was locked from the inside. Eleven-forty-seven. He took out his pistol and shot the knob right off the door. Ellena or whoever else was around would hear this, but it didn't make a difference now. He tried the door again. It still didn't give. So he kicked it and kicked it again until he was able to push his hand through the hole he'd made above the lock, and opened it from inside.

Once on the floor, he headed for the only light coming from the east wing. The door was ajar. He pushed it open a little more in order to step inside. It was then that he heard the click of her gun.

"What are you doing here, Sami?"

She didn't sound surprised but tired, as if she had strength enough for only one activity and nothing in her design included him right now. She put her gun on the desk. She was standing next to the window behind a long office desk. The room was barren. It was obvious that no one had really gotten around to using the place ever since the Americans had handed it back to the Iranian government. It was cold in here, too. She wore a long down jacket and her head and neck were covered with a long flower-patterned shawl. Dejection was becoming to her, lending her a slightly roughed-up version of the Audrey Hepburn look. Lying on the desk was a half-eaten sandwich, an open half-pint bottle of whisky, and a pen. Sami imagined her having sat here all day with her whisky and sandwich, thinking up poems in her head and waiting for the Colonel to show up. No sign of the cassette player, though.

"We have to get out of here, Ellena."

"And go where? Iran? Syria? Libya? Lebanon? No thanks, Sami, I think I've already worn out all my welcomes."

"So you plan to blow things up instead? You think that will open up some new doors for us?"

"I don't plan to blow anything up," she said quietly without looking his way. They could hear the last second countdown of the year from up here. Ten, nine, eight . . . Sami's heart froze for an instant. He wanted to close his eyes but couldn't.

The ball had fallen, the people were screaming, it was a new year, and nothing had changed.

He said, "Ellena, he's not coming."

She turned to him. "So he sent you here to get rid of me, huh? You realize you'll be next, don't you?"

He was quiet for a while. Then he answered, "It's true that

he sent me. But I've only come to *get* you. To take you away with me. I love you."

She laughed. "Don't be absurd."

"It's no more absurd than you and me standing in this godforsaken place right now."

"So where is it you propose to take me with you, Sami?" she asked wearily.

"I don't know. I can work things out. Maybe when I get a good working relationship with the Americans . . ."

She laughed harder this time, not letting him finish his sentence. "You really *are* absurd tonight." Then with a more serious voice she added, "You don't have a clue why I'm here tonight. Do you, Sami?"

"I have an idea."

"Oh yes, you have an idea. An idea like this image of me you have in your head. American woman gone astray, right? Sort of like the mother you never knew."

"Shut up!"

"You still believe I started working for your people out of some fantastic sense of duty to the world, don't you? You even have a name for it, the Florence Nightingale syndrome. And you think now that I'm sulky and disappointed because you guys are teaming up with the Americans, I want to bring the whole house down. You might as well blame it all on my cunt and my bloody period, you patronizing bastard."

"Ellena, now is not the time for this talk," he said unconvincingly. "Let's just get out of here."

"Sami, you poor idiot!" She started to laugh hysterically. "I've been working for the Libyans all along."

"Stop! I'm sick of it."

"No, sickness is a luxury you can't afford right now. You have to listen."

She told him. Starting with Europe one more time and the young American woman who had gone there seeking adventure. Sarajevo, yes. The dead Algerian boy in that photograph, yes again. "Sami, I didn't tell you any lies but only fed you the truth in bits and pieces." Was he surprised? Not really? Well, he ought to be. For she had been the only member of her Paris Algerian cell the French hadn't eventually fingered and riddled with bullets. And no, she hadn't joined her Algerians because of some maniacal fascination with those Front Islamique du Saluti bozos. She'd joined because she was in love, and when you're in love, things happen. It hadn't exactly been an easy ride with some of the more zealous entities she'd had to deal with at times. But she'd gotten hooked on the promise of adventure, even if utter boredom did clog up whole chunks of her time once in the game . . . because—and here was the real catch—because she could at least pretend to herself that the quality of her boredom was different from that of the average sales girl in New York.

Afterwards, she thought she could come back to the States and resume this other life, as if her year in Europe had been mere dreamtime. Retired terrorist on permanent loan to herself. But the respite had lasted only until that morning when the dreaded knock had come at her door at the place off the rue de Tanger. The bearded Libyan stranger had informed her that her supposed Algerian splinter cell had been in Libyan pay all along. Confusing? Yes, of course. But not improbable, especially when there was a bearded little Libyan sitting in your kitchen telling you to pack your bags, now you belonged to them.

Then what? Then Sarajevo because the Libyans were looking to score points anywhere they could. They wanted her to hang around and see if she'd get picked up by anyone from either side. When the Colonel finally threw her a line, they were overjoyed with how her case was turning out. And once they found out that the Office was a layer deeper within the labyrinth of the Iranian intelligence, they were even happier. Now they had a direct line on who was screwing who in Tehran. It meant a lot to them. Eventually the Office sent her back to the States and made her their point man in New York. In the meantime the Libyans had her reporting whatever she could on the Office back to Tripoli. Harmless stuff until now, really. Except for the uncomfortable feeling that the Libyans had strong-armed her into becoming an operative for two Middle Eastern countries she'd never even set foot in before.

"Do you believe me, Sami?"

"I don't know," he said, as he squeezed unconsciously on the grip of the pistol still dangling from his sweaty right hand. "I don't know why the Libyans would be so interested in what we're up to."

"Don't be silly!" For instance, she told him, when the Libyans had found out that the Office was planning to eliminate Section Nineteen, they weren't amused at all, since Section Nineteen's politics were much more in tune with Tripoli's than were the Office's. But they were willing to swallow the scheme as long as the Office kept Musavi and Havelock for partners. Musavi was a Libyan, after all, and Havelock had been working with the Libyans for a long time. So they figured that an alliance between those two and the Office would feed them the lowdown on Tehran more than ever before. They'd miscalculated abominably, of course. The Colonel had turned around and double-crossed Musavi and Havelock at the first opportunity. By the time the Libyans realized that the intention of the Office all along had been to team up with the Americans, it was way too late to back out. All they could do now was try to save the situation. So they'd given the bomb to Ellena and tasked her to detonate it in a building belonging specifically to the Office. Blowing up the cassette player here would produce two results. It would put a question mark on the previous cassette player bombings that had been blamed so unequivocally on the Libyans, and it would keep the Iranians and the Americans from reaching an understanding for a long time to come.

"So is that why you've come here tonight? To blow this place up?" he asked her anxiously.

She looked at him with what he could only interpret as disbelief.

"Sami, why would I want to call up the Colonel and give him a warning if I was going to do that?"

"I don't know. Why would you?"

"For the same reason I shot Havelock's Arab up in Harlem. For you."

He believed her and he didn't.

Now she was saying she hadn't wanted to do what the Libyans wanted of her. But she realized that the only way to get out of it was to first get dropped by the Office altogether. If she could make the Libyans see that the Office had dropped her as an agent, then they would no longer think her capable of pulling off the blowup job at the building site. It was a terrible gamble and far too dependent on other people's reactions toward her. But it was the only bluff she could think of that might allow her to break free from both the Office and

Libyan intelligence at one stroke so that the two of them, Sami and Ellena, could turn over a new leaf, together. What she had done then was to contact the Colonel and pretend she was fed up, that she wanted no part of the new cooperation between the Office and American intelligence.

"And you thought he would let you walk away just like that?" Sami asked incredulously.

"No. But as I said, it was a chance I had to take for the two of us, you and me."

They stood watching each other in silence. Outside, things seemed to have quieted down fast.

Sami asked, "Ellena, why have you come here tonight, then? Why are you here if all you wanted was to walk away?"

"Just to see it through. I told the Colonel I wanted a meeting. To have a tête-à-tête, so to speak. I wanted to persuade him not to hunt me . . . us down."

He wanted to believe her, desperately.

He said, "Nur is dead, Ellena. All this time you've known he was on to us and still you left me guessing. Why?"

"Sorry, Sami. I'm sorry I've had to straddle the fence this long. But Nur was a phantom to me. I was getting mixed signals from both Tehran and Tripoli. That's why I had to take Zaheri out; I had to prove to the Office I could be counted on. I figured somebody was trying to test me. But I didn't know who. You forget one thing: at the end of the day, I *am* an American. By the time you showed up in New York I'd already figured out I was caught in the middle of something way beyond me. I just didn't know where my loyalties were supposed to lie."

"So you took the cassette player from Nur and agreed to install it here for him? Is that what you did?"

"That's not it at all. The cassette player, *that* I got from the Libyans, like I told you. If you looked inside it, which you did, you must have noticed it was neutralized. I had planned to use its existence to get Nur to come here tonight."

He was baffled. "Why?"

She looked at him with a face like stone. "To kill him. Why else?"

"To kill him?"

"Sami, Nur is—*was*—a cold-blooded killer of innocent people. I wanted him out as much as you did. But I had to have a reasonable alibi."

He was starting to catch her drift. By killing Nur in this office, she'd be tagging the Office for his murder. The Arabs then would have no cause to suspect Ellena herself of foul play. It was like killing two birds with one stone.

He said, "All this time you never really trusted me, did you?"

She said, "And you're returning that favor now."

His mind wandered for a second. He imagined he could reach out across the space that separated them from each other and caress her face. He wanted to believe all that she'd told him and at the same time his pistol grip was a reminder that there probably wasn't a thick line between writing a poem and telling a lie.

On the other side of the room she stood quite still for a while and then made a sudden resolute move downwards as if she wanted to touch something on the floor. A spark went off in Sami's brain.

"Ellena, don't!"

She gave him a quizzical look for just a moment. The shot caught her on the upper right side of her back as she was bending down. It sent her rolling into the seat behind her, where she fell to the floor.

Sami ran to her. He was crying now. "I'm sorry . . . I didn't mean to . . . I thought—"

She tried to lift herself from the floor but fell back down. "Give me your hand." He reached under her and lifted her up.

"Oh, Sami!"

"Don't talk. I'm going to get you to a hospital."

"Sami . . ."

"Shhh! Don't talk. Tell me where it is. Is it in here?" He pointed to the desk drawer by his foot.

"Where's what?"

His heart fell. "The thing—the bomb."

He was getting her blood through her jacket now and over his hand. She was breathing hard.

"It's not here, Sami. I didn't bring it. I never meant to . . ." She was going out on him. She smiled distantly and closed her eyes. "You know, to get shot like this . . . it's a good thing you say you love me or I'd *really* be in trouble, huh?"

"Shhh! Come on." He put both their guns in his jacket and tried to pull her over him.

"My book," she mumbled.

"What?"

"My notebook."

He looked down and saw her poetry notebook lying on the floor. That was what she'd been reaching for when he'd shot her. He picked the notebook up and put it in her hand.

"Hold on to this, okay? Press hard. I'm going to have to walk us down."

It went slow. *Slow!* More and more he could feel the

warmth of her blood on his hand. How would they ever get out? A few times she muttered, "Love," like some outdated mantra and giggled breathlessly. By the time they finally got to the first floor, he was drenched in sweat. He set her on the steps for a minute.

"Ellena, look at me. Look at me, Ellena! Here"—he put his own jacket over her too now—"you're going to hold on to me and we're going to walk out of here together. You understand?"

She didn't respond, but he could tell she was still hanging on. He lifted her up again, this time wrapping her arm over his neck and holding on tight. Then he pulled on the door that was open to the ground floor.

One moment he was stepping through a door with Ellena on his arm and the next he saw a line of blue bodies pointing at him from the hall.

"Put your hands up and face the wall!"

It took a second, and then, gingerly so she wouldn't fall, he leaned her into the wall and started to draw the pistol. When the first bullet struck him he rolled his eyes and caught a glimpse of flashing lights on the outside. The second bullet brought him to his knees. He looked up again and thought he saw the night watchman he'd tied up earlier pointing at him through the glass doors.

"Put your hands up!"

He looked up at Ellena and smiled. Her eyes were wide open now and she was looking back and forth from Sami to the cops. He reached to grasp her hand, as if all that had happened was he'd fallen and was now about to get up to continue their walk. His gun was still hanging limply from his other hand. The movement made him lose control of it for a second, and automatically he tried to right himself with the hand holding the weapon. Ellena turned away and then turned back. "*No!*" She dived to put herself between Sami and the policemen and the next volley of shots spattered two sets of brain matter over the back wall.

"Son of a bitch!" a burly cop said to no one in particular. "What a way to start the year!"

EPILOGUE

ON THE AFTERNOON of January 6, James Saunders, FBI Special Agent in Charge of the New York field office, a decorated marine with two tours of duty in Nam behind him, was not in a particularly good mood. He couldn't give a rat's ass about how many rag-headed sand niggers from the Middle East killed each other off. The more the merrier, he thought. And lately they seemed to be on the more side. But he was still trying to develop leads about the air force base bombing in Saudi Arabia and he needed all the cooperation he could get from those NYPD juvenile delinquents. What he got instead was a police commissioner who got up in front of the cameras and proclaimed that a minor (oh, he liked that touch: *minor*) terrorist plot had been foiled in Manhattan in recent weeks and that the New York City Police Department was working extra hard to pool their resources with the federal authorities to lead the fight in combating domestic and international terrorism in the United States.

"Who is it?" he called out. At that moment Agnes McCafferty, lovely and buxom Agnes McCafferty, walked into the room with a cup of coffee for the boss. Give Agnes a compliment about her looks and you were likely to face a firing squad from the thought police lurking in every nook nowadays. Whoever said Hoover's times were bad? *This* was bad.

He was Jimmy to his very close friends and to a few of his surviving marine buddies. Jimmy had spent seventeen years in counterintelligence playing cat and mouse with the Russians in Washington and the Maryland countryside. To Jimmy the Russians were competition, not enemies. It had been a game of give-and-take and of chess played at very high stakes. For every Ivan he'd entrapped, there had been countless hours of planning, of nights sitting outside of the Soviets' GRU compound in D.C., of occasional vodka binges with men you knew you could learn to love if only the world was run a little differently, of phone calls coming at odd hours of the night, of playing baby-sitter to traitors and would-be traitors and would-be would-be traitors. True, the game had been irritating at times, but he'd loved it. Nowadays he often recalled the actor Edward G. Robinson in that old John Huston movie *Key Largo:* "Maybe we'll have Prohibition back some day." Yeah, maybe. Maybe Ivan would draw the curtain shut once more and say, "Hey, it was all a joke, a mistake. What do you say we start over again?" Maybe! But for now this Special Agent in Charge had to deal with the quite evidently thick-in-the-head Arabs and Iranians and every other Joe Blow who took it into his head to search the Internet for instructions on how to make homemade bombs.

The NYPD had come up with zilch. The Joint Task Force was twiddling its collective thumb and pointing the finger at people in Washington. In the meantime every lead they received told him only one thing: Langley had its dirty fingerprints all over the place. Try and tell this to *anyone* and you'd have the whole world barking at your doorstep. No way! This was supposed to be the age of smooth cooperation between the agencies. If Langley had anything to contribute, they would. Oh, is that so? Then what about the girl's apartment that had been thoroughly cleaned out, as if no one had lived there in years? And the Iranian? Some cock-and-bull story about a quick Moslem burial and before you knew it the body was gone.

"The hell with it!"

Jimmy Saunders finished his coffee. He put on his hat and coat and braced himself for the cold weather outside. It was Tuesday. At 6:30 P.M. sharp on Tuesdays he met with Larry Walfish for golf practice at the Chelsea Piers. Larry was not only an old pal from their high school days, but also an NYPD lieutenant with twenty-two years on the force. So if Larry could help, he would. But was there really a chance any of this could be tied in with the Dhahran bombing in Saudi Arabia? Jimmy didn't know. Then ought he press Larry about the New Year's Eve incident on 47th Street? No, not today. Jimmy Saunders could not remember which *old pal* owed a favor to the other these days. He walked past Agnes McCafferty's desk and offered a castrated smile her way. Old Ivan was a better game than the new Mohammed, hands down. Maybe after he retired next year he'd write a book about just that and other areas of his expertise. He'd open a business security firm right here in booming New York City and he'd give his opinions to interested journalists as an old Cold Warrior. That definitely beat chasing after the Mohammed mirage. Hands down.